Rockin' Autumn

SAMANTHA MICHAELS

SAMANTHA MICHAELS BOOKS

First and foremost, this book is dedicated to the readers!
Thank you to my husband and our dog for putting up with me. Thank
you to my PA Zoe and my author besties JJ & Lala!! Thank you to all the
amazing authors and those that support authors for being an inspiration!

Chapter One

Damien

"Babe, you ready to head down to the club?"

"You bet!"

Lexi put me in charge of the design part of the renovations and I have a lot of ideas. Lexi takes the staff to the back for a meeting while I gather up the construction crew.

"Thank you all for being part of this project. Not only is this my fiancée's dream, but also a way to honor her friend's memory. I want to keep the bar and kitchen areas intact, with some minor upgrades. The biggest part of our project is expanding the building to add room for the bookstore. One last thing I want to say. I hired this crew because of your reputation and experience, so I won't be one of those annoying micromanagers. You have the specs and the plans, so I'm trusting you to it. Of course, if at any time there's a question or a decision, you have my cell."

The crew's foreman, Mickey, thanked me for that. He told me a couple horror stories about past projects and how they were treated. It's awful the way some people behave. I head to the back and call Palermo's. I order enough pizza to feed the crew and ask for them to be delivered around noon. I then wait for Lexi in her office. I can hear the rest of the staff meeting as she left the door partially open.

"Finally, I want to thank you all for agreeing to stay on. I'd like to open it up for any questions." Lexi says.

"First, thanks for keeping all of us. We were worried when we heard the club had a new owner. Will we be expanding the staff to cover the new parts of the club or will we be expected to work longer hours?"

"Great question, Cassie. I certainly will be hiring more staff. I'm a firm believer in work-life balance, so I want all of you to have a life outside of the club. Any other questions?"

"I have one more, if that's okay?" Cassie says.

"Yes, of course." Lexi says.

"Would you consider hiring a permanent DJ? I have a perfect candidate."

"Yes, I would like to, so let's chat after the meeting. Any other questions?"

Nobody else asks Lexi anything, so I hear her wrap up the meeting.

"You'll all be paid your full salary while we're closed for renovations, so please, go enjoy this beautiful summer weather. I have contact information for all of you, so I'll keep in touch via group texts. As soon as I have an approximate grand re-opening date, I'll inform everyone."

I hear the staff applaud before they head out. Lexi comes into the office and smiles when she sees me. Damn that woman is so sexy. I still can't believe she's the same shy woman who wouldn't even look at me in the club. I owe Dave a big juicy steak for his part in this. Lexi sits on the desk and wags her finger at me, so I walk over and stand between her legs.

"Mmmm, I love my sexy man."

Before I can respond, I feel her lips on mine. Her tongue is eagerly exploring my mouth and I'm getting hard. I want to take her right here on this desk. She flashes me a dirty look and jumps off the desk. She bends at the waist leaning her chest on the desk. I watch her hands rub her sexy ass.

"Damien, I want you to take my pussy from behind. Right here, right now. And it better be hard and fast. I want you so damn bad."

"Shit, woman, you never stop surprising me."

I reach around and slide her jeans and panties down to her ankles. She steps out of them then reaches down to take her sneakers off, but I stop her.

"Leave them on, babe. You look so cute like that."

She laughs then removes her own shirt and bra. Fuck, she's so damn hot. I can't believe how much her standing there naked except for socks and sneakers is turning me on. I make sure the office door is locked then strip myself naked where she can see me. She licks her lips when I free the beast.

"First, I want you up on the desk."

She gets back up on the desk. I walk over and spread her legs wide. Damn, I never get tired of seeing that sweet pussy. Her scent intoxicates me and I'm desperate for a taste. I slide my tongue into her folds and lick her hard. I stop and suck on her clit. I feel her body quaking and I know I have her close. I slide a couple of fingers inside her to make sure she's ready for her pounding. Of course she is, this dirty, insatiable sex goddess I love so much. I keep sucking her clit until her body shakes and she screams.

I help her off the desk. She leans over again, her legs still shaking from her orgasm, and holds on tight. I grab my dick and guide it inside of her sweet pussy with one hard thrust. She groans loudly as I pound her hard. She takes every inch of me deep inside as my balls slap against that sexy ass. Fuck she feels so good and damn what a view. I love seeing her bent over the desk like this. I give her ass a light smack and she moans.

"Fuck me harder, baby. I can take it."

"First, I want you back up on that desk. I want to watch you take me."

I lift her back onto the desk and open her legs. She doesn't take her eyes off my face as I slide inside her. I lock eyes with her while we fuck, and it's so damn hot. I watch as she teases her own clit while she takes her pounding. Her gorgeous tits are bouncing hard. Nothing compares to watching her like this. My beautiful goddess. I lose all control as I fill her, groaning as I come inside of her.

I lift her off the desk and carry her over to the couch. We're sitting there basking in the afterglow when I hear a knock on the office door. I've never been more grateful I remembered to lock it.

"Mr. St. James, we need to ask you a couple of questions." Mickey says.

"I'll be right down."

I go back to the couch just as Lexi loses it. She starts laughing so hard, tears are pouring down her face.

"What the hell, woman?"

"I can't believe we just did that. We could have gotten caught."

"So what! You own this place now. And you're a sight to behold, especially naked."

"Still, I don't want an audience. I cherish these moments with you. They're for us only."

"I understand, but you know us dudes! I earn major cool points for landing a woman as hot as you."

"Damien! That better not be all I mean to you!"

"No way in hell, woman. If that's all you were to me, you wouldn't have that ring on your finger. I love you more than life itself."

"Oh, Damien."

"For now though, let's get dressed so we can see what Mickey needs."

We head downstairs. Mickey needs to know how we want the bookshelves set up, so Lexi takes over and shows him while I wait. Once we're done, we head home. After we have dinner, we feed and walk the dogs.

The rest of the days leading up to Labor Day go by fast. Mickey keeps the crew on target and they finish a couple of days early. Lexi has finished her hiring, so we gather the staff along with the construction crew. I sit and watch as Lexi addresses them.

"Welcome to BYOB! First, I want to thank Mickey and his amazing team for their hard work. Everything looks amazing and I'm beyond impressed that you finished ahead of schedule. I also want to thank the staff and welcome our new members. Thank you all for being patient. We're a couple of days away from the opening. I have deliveries coming today of books and alcohol, so we can get the bar and the book shelves stocked. But before we get to work on the finishing touches, let's celebrate."

Lexi looks over at me, so I join her up front. "Catering staff have just finished setting up lunch in the kitchen area. Please, everyone, go help yourselves to some food. You've all earned this celebration."

Everyone eats then gets to work. Mickey and his team stay to help us with the rest of the work and we get everything finished Sunday afternoon, the day before the big opening. Lexi spoke to Dean and secured Stardust to play. We're expecting quite the party. Lexi and I do one last look over once everyone else is gone, then lock up and head home. We're both exhausted and we head to bed early.

The opening was amazing and we had a bigger crowd than we anticipated. Stardust was incredible as always. Doug's parents attended for a short time and they were pleased with what Lexi did. We asked Mickey to put a tribute area together to honor Doug and Meg. Lexi's on cloud nine and anxious to start planning some events. I'm anxious to start planning our wedding...

Chapter Two

Lexi

"**N**ew Year's Eve is perfect!" I squeal.

"I was hoping you would like that, baby," Damien says. "We just need to decide where."

"Then that's our mission today."

"I hope that's not our only mission, babe?"

"Meaning?"

"Mission Get Naked should always be a priority." Damien growls as he grabs me and pulls me against him.

"Mmmm, I'm all for starting our day with a bang." I laugh.

In about two seconds, Damien has me out of my pajamas and his head's between my thighs. His masterful tongue quickly sends me soaring. He slides up my body, fucks me hard and fast, quickly exploding inside me. Fuck, I never get tired of that!

After we shower and get dressed, we head to the kitchen. Damien puts the coffee on then gets breakfast ready for the dogs while I take them out to do their business. I look over at Judd's empty farm and wonder how he's doing. He left so abruptly and never told us why, so I can't help but fear that something bad happened. I hope he comes back, as I'm still convinced he and Mel belong together.

Maggie barks. I look over and see both dogs standing at the door, so I let them in. They run to their food bowls and empty them like they haven't eaten in a month. Damien hands me a cup of coffee, as always fixed exactly the way I love it.

"You know, you two get fed twice a day, every day." I say to Maggie and Dave. Damien laughs after watching them race to see who could empty their bowl first.

"What about you? What would you like for breakfast?" I ask Damien.

"Well, I already had my favorite breakfast, so maybe just an omelet and toast?" he asks.

"I could just sit on the counter and let you taste my sweet pussy again." I tease and Damien almost spits out his coffee.

"Damn, I have the naughtiest woman."

"Damn right, you do. You definitely awakened her. I can't believe how shy I was when we first got together. Spring was quite the awakening for this girl."

"It was my pleasure, baby."

I smile as I get to work on the omelets while Damien takes care of the toast. When everything's ready, Damien pours two more cups of coffee and we sit down to eat. After we're done and cleaned up, we head over to Judd's farm to take care of his animals. We're just getting back home when I see Mel pull into our driveway. She does not look happy.

"Hey, girl, what's going on?" I ask my friend.

"Can we go out back?" Mel asks, tears filling her eyes.

I put an arm around Mel and we walk out back while Damien goes inside. Mel sits down and puts her head in her hands. I join her, and put a hand on her arm.

"Talk to me, sweetie." I say.

"I visited my mom on Saturday," she says.

"What did Trish do?" I think back to some of the times Mel came to me in tears after dealing with her bitch of a younger sister.

"She asked me for money. When I said no, she started screaming at me about me not having kids. She told me it was punishment for being

7

a cold-hearted bitch. I hate myself for it, but I burst into tears. All that accomplished was provoking her to bring up my lack of love life. I'm so damn tired of being a loser." She says, tears streaming down her face.

I'm so angry, I could spit, but that won't help my friend. I slide my chair closer and give her a hug. She held on tight for quite a while then pulled away.

"I'm sorry." She says quietly.

"For what?" I ask.

"Dumping all this on you. We should be talking about your wedding."

"Stop that now! You're my best friend and I love you. You had me first and you always will. I promise you one thing, Trish will NOT be invited to the ceremony."

That gets a small smile out of Mel. All of a sudden we hear two barks and look at the sliding door. Both dogs are standing there, noses pressed against the glass. Mel starts laughing. Her laugh is infectious and I can't help but laugh too. I get up and let the dogs out. Maggie runs right to Mel and lays her head on Mel's leg.

"She always knows." Mel says.

"That she does." I agree.

As she absentmindedly rubs Maggie's head, I see Mel look over at Judd's ranch. "Have you heard from him?" she asks.

"Not a word. I'm worried about him." I answer.

"I know. But, now, onto my favorite topic. Have you lovebirds picked a date yet? Or a venue?"

Smiling wide, I answer, "New Year's Eve. I know it seems soon, but we only want something small. The venue, no clue."

"What about the club?"

"That's perfect! Thank you. Now, I need to ask you something."

"Ask away."

"Will you be my best woman?"

"Don't you mean maid of honor?"

"I hate that term. You're my best woman!"

"I love you and of course I accept. You are my one and only sister."

"I feel the same way. Love you bunches."

"I gotta run. Let me know when you're ready to go dress shopping!" Mel says.

"Probably soon. Call me anytime you need me." I say.

"Even if you and Damien are gettin' it on?" Mel asks, laughing.

"Well, okay almost anytime..." I joke.

I walk her to her car. When I return to the backyard, Damien's sitting at the table with two glasses of iced tea. I join him as we sit and watch the dogs play in the yard. I start giggling and Damien looks at me.

"What's funny, baby?" he asks.

"I was just watching the dogs play and thinking that once we get married, they'll be siblings." I say.

"You're just too cute, woman! Different topic, what was up with Mel?"

"I can't really say much, it's her story to tell, but her sister is horrible."

"That really sucks."

"Yeah. I think a lot of it is jealousy, but that doesn't make it any easier for Mel to deal with. She asked me if we'd heard from Judd and it's obvious that she likes him."

"I hope whatever happens, things work out for him." Damien says.

"Me too." I say.

"So, while Mel was here, I may have arranged a special surprise for tonight. No questions, as I won't answer them. You just have to wait and see." Damien says.

"Not even a little hint?"

"No way, woman, and if you ask again, there will be consequences."

I stick my tongue out and say, "Not even a little hint?"

He gives me a stern look then gets up. Next thing I know, I'm over his shoulder and he walks toward the pond.

"Damien St. James, you better not do what I think you're going to do." I warn.

"I told you there'd be consequences."

I never get a chance to respond before I'm soaked from head to toe. I'm sitting in the pond, trying to be mad, but when Maggie and Dave jump in with me, all I can do is laugh. Damien turns his attention away for a minute, so I tug on his leg and pull him into the pond.

"Woman!" He pulls me close and kisses me hard.

"You deserved that."

"Yeah, guess I did," he laughs. "Let's get the two furries dried out then grab a shower."

After our showers we hung around the house. I kept waiting for my surprise. Finally, Damien ended the torture. We loaded the dogs up in the car and he started driving. After a while, we pulled up to a farm with a large barn.

"I was chatting with the guys from Stardust a while back and borrowed this idea from Andy. I hope you like it," Damien said after he parked. "Join me in the back seat."

We get in the backseat with Maggie and Dave. An image appeared on the side of the barn. I squealed when the opening theme of Pretty in Pink started.

"You are getting so lucky tonight!" I say.

After we get home from the movie, we go right to bed, and it's a wonder we didn't need a fire extinguisher when we were done!

Chapter Three

Damien

"Anything on the agenda today?" I ask Lexi while we're eating breakfast outside.

"I'm going down to BYOB this morning to check on things." she says.

The face of the man I saw after the opening appears in my mind. "I'll go with you, in case you need help."

"Help with what? Getting fucked on my desk again?" Lexi teases.

"Or the couch, I'm not picky."

"Trying to take a page out of Mikael's book? From what Alex has told me, Mikael and Hannah spent A LOT of time in her office with the door locked!"

"I like the way he thinks. Seriously, though, I'll help you with the work you need to do."

"Sounds good. I only planned on being there for a couple of hours then I was thinking we could take a drive with the doggies."

"Sounds like the perfect day to me."

Some of the trees are just starting to turn colors and there's the slightest chill in the air. This is completely different from what I'm used to in LA, but I find it comforting. LA can be stifling in more ways than one. Plus, on those cold days, I can curl up with the sexiest woman on earth.

We head down to the club so Lexi can get her work done. When we get inside, I take a look at the bar to see if we're running low on anything while Lexi goes upstairs to her office. I check the list of what Lexi wants on hand of each bottle, and note what she needs to order. Of course, all I really want is to get my ass up those stairs and get her naked on the couch. I grab the inventory list and head up to her office. She has the door shut, so I knock.

"Who is it?" Lexi asks.

"Cock-o-gram!" I say.

"I'm busy. Could you come back later?" she asks.

"What? You don't want to see the world's sexiest man get naked for you?"

"Oh, I didn't realize Shemar Moore was here..." she laughs.

I swing the door open and see Lexi sitting at her desk with a big smile on her gorgeous face. "You're in big trouble now." I say.

"You think so, huh?" she says, sticking her tongue out at me.

I walk over to the desk and spin her chair so she's facing me. I put my hand out, but she ignores me and crosses her arms across her chest. I lock the office door as I walk by and walk over to the couch. I watch her as I get naked and sit down on the couch. My dick stands at full attention, aching to be inside her. She turns her focus back to her laptop, as if there's not a naked man with a hard-on sitting on the couch.

"Woman, get that ass over here and sit on my cock." I command.

"And if I don't?"

"I guess I'll be forced to take things into my own hands."

"Stroke it for me, sexy." she teases.

Oh, so this is how she wants to play. Fine. I'll call her bluff! I grab my dick, gaze into her eyes and run my hand up and down. She licks her lips then takes her ponytail down. She shakes her hair loose and I almost shoot my load. I watch her get up from her chair and sit on the edge of her desk. She opens her jeans, spreads her legs and slides a hand down her pants. I can tell from her soft moans exactly what she's doing.

She finally gets up and walks over to me. She removes her sneakers and socks then slides her jeans and panties down. She slowly lifts her shirt and removes her bra. She stands in front of me. She takes my hand off my dick, straddles me, and slowly lowers her wet pussy on my cock, taking every last inch of me inside her.

"Fuck, I want you so bad." she says.

She bounces up and down hard and fast, causing the couch to move across the floor. Damn, this woman's so fucking incredible. She cries out as I feel her body quake. She comes hard around me and keeps bouncing. She comes a second time, screaming even louder this time as I empty inside her. She collapses against me, her chest heaving. She crushes her lips to mine. We break our kiss when we hear a knock at the door.

"Yes." Lexi calls out.

"It's Cassie. Is everything okay up here?"

"Of course, why?" Lexi asks.

"I could hear banging on the ceiling below and wanted to make sure."

"All good here!" she says as I try unsuccessfully to stifle a laugh.

"Okay." Cassie says. We hear her walk downstairs.

"Ummm, I guess we should get dressed and go down there." Lexi says.

Her face is bright red. I'm trying to figure out if it's from fucking me or from almost getting caught.

"Before we do, I need to tell you something." I say, pulling her close.

"Oh, and what might that be?"

"That was so fucking hot, woman!"

"Mmmm, it sure was. Nothing feels quite like having that sexy dick inside me."

I kiss her hard then say, "Just you wait until later!" I give her a light smack on her sexy ass then start getting dressed. She follows suit then closes up the office. We walk downstairs and see Cassie with a few members of the staff. We're met with a round of applause, so it's pretty safe to say everyone knows what the noise was! I look at Lexi and her eyes are glued to the floor.

I walk over to the bar and hand Cassie the inventory list, so she can place the order. Once we're done, we head out to another round of applause and a few catcalls. By the time we reach my car, we're both laughing our asses off. When we get home, we get the dogs loaded in the car and hit the open road. One of my favorite things about living here is the lack of traffic. After the pure hell of LA traffic, this is a welcomed change.

I get to a remote location and pull the car off the road into a field. We proceed to give the dogs quite a show bent over the hood of the car. It's a damn good thing dogs don't talk, or everyone would know some damn dirty secrets about us. We're on our way home when Lexi tells me she's starving.

"For food or something else?" I ask.

"Down, boy." she says.

I hear movement in the backseat and see that Dave is now laying down. I laugh and say, "He may have listened, but I'm not gonna. Just wait until I get you home."

Lexi laughs and I hear that cute snort I love so much. There couldn't be a woman more perfect for me. As we're driving, she spots a roadside eatery with picnic tables. There's a sign that says leashed pets are welcome, so we stop there. Lexi takes the dogs to a table while I order dinner for us. After we eat, we finish our drive. Once we get the dogs situated, we never leave the bedroom until morning.

Chapter Four

Lexi

After a lazy morning lounging in bed, we grab showers then enjoy brunch out back. I love watching the dogs run and play. It won't be long before the trees start dropping their leaves, something Maggie loves. She's one of those crazy dogs that likes to jump into big piles of them. I throw a tennis ball down and both dogs get the zoomies. I never get tired of watching them.

I look at my watch, as I need to be at the club in an hour for some deliveries I need to sign for. After we finish eating, I clean up while Damien stays out back with the dogs. After they finish running, the dogs come up to the door, so Damien brings them in. Both dogs run to their water bowls and leave a small flood on the kitchen floor.

"I swear they are the two messiest drinkers ever." I say.

"I think you might be right." Damien says.

"I'm going to head down to the club in a little while. There's a couple deliveries I need to sign for and I want to see if I've had any bites on my social media post."

"What post?"

"I would love to have some indie authors come and sign autographs at the bookstore."

"That's a great idea. I'd love to thank some of those romance authors that made you so dirty-minded."

"Excuse me? I'm as pure as they come!" I say, barely able to keep a straight face.

"This from the woman who rode my cock in her office yesterday?"

He tickles my stomach and I pull away, racing into the living room. He chases me so I start doing laps around the couch. Apparently, the dogs think this is a game they should be included in and I suddenly have two flashes of fur tearing around the couch. Damien and I get out of the way before we get knocked on our asses. After a few laps, they race over to their water bowls and leave me another flood to clean up.

"How about I come with you again, as I have a surprise for you afterwards?"

"Okay, but no office shenanigans today, as delivery trucks are coming."

"They get to come but I don't? No fair, woman!"

"There'll be plenty of time later for sex. You know how much I love that sexy dick."

"Fuck."

We get down to the club and a few minutes later the delivery trucks pull in. One of them has the air hockey and foosball tables I ordered. The other is a food delivery. Once we have all the food put away and the games setup, I go up to the office so I can check social media. I respond to the couple of authors that have already responded, then head back downstairs. We drive to Lancaster and Damien parks in front of a store called Barstools and Billiards.

"What are we doing here?" I ask.

"I was thinking we could do something with the empty basement. How about a bar and a pool table?" Damien says.

"I love the idea. Could we also get a big screen TV to hang?"

"Absolutely, plus I want some type of stereo system."

"I love that idea. I love playing pool, especially nine ball." I say.

"I actually had something else in mind for the table..." Damien says.

I smile. "Let me guess, it involves us being naked?"

"Damn right, woman. I'm going to fuck you like you've never been fucked before."

"Mmmm, Damien."

One of the store's employees approaches us. "May I help you?" he asks.

"Yes, I'd like to purchase one of your slate billiard tables." Damien says.

"Great choice. They're much sturdier." he says with a slight smirk.

Oh shit, I think to myself. We really need to learn how to be a little more quiet. I look at Damien and his cheeks are red. Oh my god, Mr. Naughtypants is actually embarrassed. I try desperately not to laugh. I try to catch his eye, but he is refusing to make eye contact. I walk to the far wall where the pool cues are hanging and try to compose myself. Damien finishes up his purchase and arranges delivery for tomorrow. He practically runs out of the store.

When we're outside, I lose the battle and I'm doubled over, laughing so hard, my face hurts. Damien puts his hands on his hips. That makes me laugh even harder and I let out a snort that would make Urkel proud.

"Okay, Miss Snorty-pants. Keep it up and no cock for you tonight." Damien says in a huff.

"Think about that," I say. "That means no pussy for you."

"Shit. But I will figure out a way to pay you back." he says.

"I dare you to try." I say.

"I never back down from a dare, woman!"

It's nearing doggy-dinner time by the time we get home. We're greeted by two furry wigglebutts. I get their dinner ready while Damien grabs our pile of menus out of the kitchen drawer. While Maggie and Dave eat, we order our favorite pepperoni pizza with extra cheese.

A little while later, I hear a car pull into the driveway. I hope it's dinner as I'm starving. Damien grabs the pizza from the delivery guy while I grab plates and return to the living room. Damien grabs a beer for himself and a wine cooler for me, then meets me in the living room. We park our butts in front of the TV and look for something to watch while we eat. We end up binging one of our favorite shows, Impractical Jokers.

"So, the pool table's coming tomorrow, right?" I ask.

"Eager are we?" he teases.

"Damn right, after what you told me you had planned."

"That's my sexy woman."

We finish eating then take the dogs for a walk. After we get back, we have a quick dessert of ice cream. I slide closer to Damien and run my hand up his leg, stopping just short of his crotch.

"I want to go to bed," I say.

""You can't be tired this early, can you?" Damien asks.

"Nope, but I am horny as hell." I say in my sexiest voice.

The next thing I know, I'm over Damien's shoulder and on my way to our bedroom.

"Strip for me, then get that sexy little smartass in bed." Damien commands.

"What do mean smartass?" I demand.

"Remember earlier? I told you I would find a way to pay you back." he says.

I get naked then lie down in the middle of bed, spreading my legs wide. He gets naked while I watch. Fuck, I love seeing that huge cock. I have a feeling I'm going to get quite a pounding from that beast tonight.

"Slide that hot ass back." he says.

I move until I'm sitting up against the headboard. He starts at my ankles and slides his hands up and down my legs. He moves to my inner thighs, lightly stroking them. I writhe, aching for him to touch my pussy, but he focuses only on my legs. So, this is my payback. He's going to torture me until I can't take it. All that does is make me even more horny for him.

He runs his tongue up and down the inside of each thigh then showers them with kisses. He sucks my inner thighs and I'm not sure how much more I can take. He moves up to my stomach, running his tongue up to my breasts. He sucks each one, teasing my nipples with his tongue. He kisses and licks my neck then moves to my lips as his body's against mine. I can feel his dick against me. I writhe, trying desperately to grind him.

"No, no, no, baby. You'll get your pleasure when I say so." he scolds.

I watch him get off the bed and leave the room. A few minutes later, he comes back with a cup in his hand. What the hell is he up to? He reaches into the cup and pulls out an ice cube. He holds it in his hand and lets freezing cold water drip on my chest. He moves down and lets water drip on my pussy. I gaze into his eyes, trying to will him into ending my torture.

He puts the rest of the ice cube in his mouth and runs his tongue between my folds. I practically fly off the bed, the sensation feels so good. He grabs another ice cube and gently teases my clit with it.

"Holy fuck, that's so good." I moan.

The ice cube quickly melts against my hot pussy. He replaces it with his tongue and I'm quickly soaring into another dimension. I explode, my entire body quivering from the ice and the pleasure he never fails to deliver. He slides up my body, lifts my hips off the bed, and slides inside me with one powerful thrust. He spends the next several hours inside me until neither of us has anything left to give.

Damien takes the dogs out for a quick potty break then locks up and comes back to bed. I wake up the next morning completely refreshed and a little sore. Yep, the good kind of sore. After we grab a quick breakfast, I head down to the club to get the payroll done. Damien stays home this time, since the pool table is scheduled to be delivered some time this morning.

Chapter Five

Damien

I'm sitting in the backyard with the dogs while Lexi's down at the club. I'm a bit on edge after yesterday. I hear a truck pull up the driveway next door. I look over and see Judd. After he parks, he walks over to the fence so I join him.

"Welcome home, man." I say.

"Thanks. It's good to be back. I can't thank you and Lexi enough for taking care of things." Judd says.

"Our pleasure. Up for a beer?"

"Sounds great. Be right over."

I go inside and grab two beers. I hear the dogs go crazy. I look out and they're both on their backs, getting belly rubs. I walk out with the two beers and put them on the table. Judd walks over and sits down.

"No Lexi?" he asks.

"She's down at the club doing some work. I'm waiting for a pool table to be delivered so I hung back."

"Been a long time since I've played."

I see a darkness sweep across Judd's face and wonder what that's all about. "Did you get everything taken care of in Texas?" I ask.

"Yeah, all good. I'm just glad to be back here. I missed ya'll."

I'm about to respond when I hear laughing. I look up and see Lexi and Mel. Lexi sees Judd and runs over. She gives him a hug, "Welcome home. How are you?"

"All good, ma'am." he says.

I see him look over at Mel, and for the first time, I realize Lexi's right. He's definitely interested in Mel. She gives him a look that I've seen on Lexi's face a lot. These two really should be together. Stop it, I yell at myself, meddling always backfires. I've told Lexi several times to just let things happen if they're meant to. I'm not sure she listens, but I try!

"Howdy ma'am." Judd says to Mel and damn if he didn't blush.

"Welcome back, Judd." Mel says, a goofy grin on her face.

I see Lexi's face light up and I give her my best "don't you get any ideas" look. She rolls her eyes at me then turns her attention back to her friend.

"I was just leaving when Mel pulled into the parking lot." Lexi announces.

"I needed a day off. Things have been hectic lately. I couldn't think of a better way to spend it than with my bestie." Mel says.

"Well, while we're all here together, how about lunch? I'll go whip up my famous chicken salad sandwiches." Lexi says.

"I'm always hungry for you, I mean your cooking." I say with a wink.

"Lunch sounds great." Judd adds.

"I'll come help you." Mel says.

"We'll be back." Lexi says as she and Mel head inside.

I turn to Judd. "Can I say something, man?"

"Of course." Judd says.

"I've seen the way you look at Mel. Why not ask her on a date?"

"It's complicated."

"Dude, she's into you too. Think about it."

"I just can't."

I drop it for now, as he clearly doesn't want to talk. We sit in an awkward silence until the ladies return with lunch and drinks for everyone. Lexi gives me a puzzled look. I know I'm going to get interrogated later. Mel sits down and Lexi passes out plates then the tray with the sandwiches. She hands Judd and I a beer and takes two wine coolers for her and Mel. Lunch is mostly filled with small talk. My cell rings and he looks down.

"The guys delivering the pool table are out front. I'll be back." I say.

I walk down and see the truck and the two delivery guys.

"Where are we headed with it?" the driver asks me.

"The basement. From the garage it's only a few steps down." I tell them.

"Sounds good. The legs are separate, so we'll assemble it once we get down there."

"Okay. Do you need me to help?"

"Nope, just open the door then show us where you want it when we have all the pieces down here."

"Got it."

I open the door and wait in the basement. All I can think about while I'm standing here is what I'm going to do with a naked Lexi on that table. A few minutes later, she and Mel come down to the basement.

"I gotta run. Thanks for lunch!" Mel says.

"Any time." Lexi says.

After Mel leaves, Lexi stands next to me. The guys bring the legs down first and I show them where I want the table. Neither of them can take their eyes off Lexi. I put an arm around her and clear my throat. They quickly get back to work and head out to grab the table top.

"My, my, a bit possessive, aren't we?" Lexi asks.

"You're mine and mine alone, baby."

"Mmmm, that's turning me on big-time." she says and grabs my ass hard.

"Stop it, woman, before you wake the snake." I laugh.

The guys come back down and finish putting the table together. They ask me to check it out for any issues before I sign the paperwork.

We follow them outside so I can sign the delivery confirmation. They hand me an envelope.

"This is a voucher for any accessories you need. Just head down to the store." the driver tells me.

"Thank you," I say as I sign the paper and hand them a tip. "What do you say we got out for dinner tonight then hit the store?"

"Sounds good. How about Palermo's?" Lexi asks.

"Let me guess, pepperoni and extra cheese?" I ask.

"Mmm, you know what I like." she purrs.

"Oh yes, I do." I say then crush my lips to hers.

We go inside to feed the dogs then take them for a quick walk before we head out. They both curl up together in their favorite corner of the living room. After we eat, we go get a set of pool sticks, balls, and all the other accessories we need then head back home. We take everything down to the basement then take the dogs out back to play. We walk down to the pond and sit down on the butterfly shaped bench Lexi bought the other day. The sun is starting to set and a chill fills the air. I feel Lexi shiver.

"Let's take the dogs inside. I wanna get in our pajamas and snuggle under a blanket with my sexy woman." I say.

We camp out on the couch until we're both exhausted. We let the dogs do their business then we all head to bed. The next morning, after breakfast, we walk Dave and Maggie down to the dog park to play. Out of nowhere, Maggie runs over to the bench where Lexi and I are sitting and starts barking. Her hair is standing on end and she shows her teeth.

"I've never seen her like this before." Lexi says, puzzled.

"I wonder what set her off?" I say.

"I have no idea. Maggie, sit."

Maggie sits and Lexi pets her. She starts to calm down a little, but there's still clearly something wrong. Maggie sits in front of Lexi looking past her and the barking starts up again. From behind us, I hear an unfamiliar female voice.

"Hello, Alexis." the woman says.

A male voice echoes, "Hello, Alexis."

I look over at her as the color drains from her face.

"Are you okay?" I ask her.

She ignores me, stands up and turns around. "What the fuck do you want?" she seethes.

"Is that any way to talk to your parents?"

Holy shit!

Chapter Six

Lexi

"That's a fucking joke." I say.

"Excuse me?" my father says.

"You stopped being my parents a long time ago."

"Why? Because we wanted you to start growing up when you turned eighteen?" my mother says.

"Fuck you. That I could have handled. No, it was all the years before that."

I feel Damien grab my hand. I wish he wasn't here right now. There's so much I've never told him. Never told anyone and I fear it's all about to come to light.

"You can't still be upset about that can you?" my asshole father says.

"Upset that you spent my whole life calling me fat, worthless, pathetic, ugly, did I miss any?"

"The truth hurts, doesn't it?" my mother says. "How could the star football player and the head cheerleader give birth to you?"

I stand there in silence, trying my hardest to choke back tears. I see

Judd pass by in his truck. He pulls into the parking lot but doesn't get out of his truck. Damien stands up next to me.

"Who is this?" my mother asks, pointing at Damien.

I'm about to answer when I hear Damien's voice. "I'm the man who's going to marry this incredible woman."

My mother doubles over in laughter, "Guess you'll need a wide aisle for her to waddle down."

"Aw, honey, look," my father says to my mother. "Big fat fatty is going to cry."

The next thing I know, my father's on his ass. I hear Judd's truck door open and close. He comes running over. I see the red mark on my father's face and realize what happened. Damien's about to run out of the park but Judd holds him back. He looks over at me and when he sees how upset I am, says to Damien, "Whoever he is, he's not worth it."

"Judd, meet my parents." I say.

Judd nods then returns his focus to keeping Damien inside the park. My father gets up and dusts himself off. My parents start to walk away.

"Wait," I say. "Before you go, I need to say something."

My parents stand there glaring at me. I take a deep breath. "You spent my entire childhood ridiculing me. It messed me up for a long time. Too long. Then, something life-changing happened. That beautiful dog," I say pointing at Dave, "knocked me on my ass. That's how Damien and I met."

"Big fucking deal." my father says.

I ignore him and continue, "Through his love and patience, he made me realize just how wrong you both were. I'm a beautiful woman inside and out. I care for the people in my life and I never treat them with anything but kindness. You tried your damnedest, but you couldn't break me."

They again start to walk away. "Oh, and one more thing. Don't ever fucking contact me again."

Damien and Judd just stand there, staring at me. "Say something." I tell them.

"Are you okay?" Damien asks.

"The old Lexi would have collapsed into a bundle of tears, but she's gone. That was long overdue and it felt damn freeing." I say.

"Why didn't you tell me any of that?"

"I couldn't bring myself to repeat the things they used to say to me."

"I'm sorry you had to go through that," Damien says. "Thanks, Judd, for keeping me from making things any worse."

"You got it," Judd says. "I'll be on my way now. Take care of your lady."

Maggie has since calmed down. I give her a pat on the head. Dogs never cease to amaze me with what they can sense. We leash up both dogs and walk back home. I can't get what happened out of my head. We get inside and Damien pulls me close. He tries to kiss me but I pull away and sit down on the couch.

"What's wrong? You never turn down a kiss from me." he says.

"Why would you want to kiss this?" I ask, pointing at myself. "I'm glad my parents showed up today to bring me back to reality."

"What do you mean?"

"You don't deserve to be stuck with a piece of garbage like me."

He walks over and sits down next to me. He looks at me and places his hands on my shoulders.

"You listen to me right now. You are none of the things your parents said. What happened to that woman back there who told them how beautiful she is?"

"I wasn't thinking straight."

"You're absolutely wrong. Please, let me remind you."

He pulls me close and I tense up. He kisses me the way he's done so many times, but I can't let myself enjoy it and I don't kiss him back. I feel the tears start, as all those painful memories fill my head. Damien tightens his embrace as I completely fall apart.

"Why the fuck did they come here? After all the hell they put me through, I'm finally happy. It's like they knew and couldn't let me enjoy it."

"I wish I could take this pain away."

"You have and I'm sorry about earlier. It's just that having all those memories come flooding back threw me for a loop."

"I understand. Seeing my dad when we went to California had the same effect."

I look into Damien's eyes and lean in for a kiss. He puts his hands

27

on my face and lays a panty-soaker on me. I run my hands down his back as we kiss. Fuck, I love this man. We finally come up for air, both of us panting.

"Take me to bed. Now! I want you to fuck me into oblivion." I growl.

"There's my woman." he says.

A few orgasms later, we're laying together when I hear Damien's cell let him know he has a text. He answers then turns the alert off.

"How does a soak in the tub before dinner sound?" he asks.

"Absolutely divine." I say.

After a luxurious bubble bath together, we throw on our jammies and head downstairs for dinner. There's a bunch of leftover Chinese food in the fridge, so we each make a plate up and park our asses in front of the TV. It's a good thing we have dogs who like to walk plus a whole lot of sex, since we tend to spend more time on the couch than we probably should.

The next morning, we're at the kitchen table eating breakfast while the dogs sleep off their morning food coma when I hear a knock at the door. Shit, I'm sitting here in sweats and my hair's in a messy bun. Damien gets up to answer the door and returns with Mel, Alex, and Dean in tow.

"We have a surprise for you," Alex says. "We're going wedding dress shopping, then lunch, then mani/pedis. Dean's gonna hangout here until we get back."

"But, I'm a mess." I say.

"You're not a mess. You look adorable." Mel says.

"I tried to tell her that." Damien says.

"You can't make me go!" I protest.

"Like hell." Damien says.

The next thing I know, I'm over his shoulder, being carried outside. Alex opens the passenger door and Damien puts me in the car then quickly closes the door. Mel gets in the backseat, laughing her ass off.

"You're a fucking dickhead." I say to Damien, laughing.

Damien bows then walks up on the porch and watches us leave. We park in front of the bridal shop and walk inside. The woman working in the store greets Alex with a hug.

"Helen, you look beautiful as always. I'd like to introduce my friends Lexi and Mel. Lexi is our bride and Mel is her best woman," Alex says. "Helen helped me find the perfect dress when I married my perfect man!"

"Thank you, Alex. I'll definitely do the same for Lexi. Would you mind if I see a picture of the groom to be?" Helen asks.

"Of course," I say. "Does that help you decide what dress would be best?"

"No. I'm just a lonely old widow and I like to check out the handsome young men you girls marry." she says with a wink.

"I wanna be like her when I grow up." I say when Helen heads to the back.

Helen brings out a few dresses for me to try. I walk to the dressing room. The first dress I try on just isn't me, but the second one is perfect. I feel like Clark Griswold when he finds the perfect Christmas tree. The dress I find is a simple silk A-line dress. The bodice criss-crosses into short sleeves, which is exactly what I wanted. I walk out to the front. Alex's jaw drops and Mel bursts into tears.

"Mel, I'm not that hideous!" I say, suddenly mortified.

"That's not why I'm crying." Mel says.

"Then what's wrong?"

"You're stunning. I've never been prouder to be your friend than I am right now."

"Mel's right. This dress is perfect for you. Damien is going to melt into a puddle when he sees you."

"Thank you all." I say as my cheeks redden. I'm not sure I'll ever be completely comfortable with compliments, especially after yesterday with my parents. I walk back to the dressing room to change back into my clothes.

"Now, what about you two?" I ask Mel and Alex.

"What color were you thinking for us?" Mel asks.

"I would really like plum." I say.

"I have just the thing. I'll be right back." Helen says.

Helen comes back a few minutes later carrying two plum dresses. She takes Mel and Alex to the dressing rooms while I wait. I have my back to the door, watching for Mel and Alex to emerge from the dressing room when I hear it open. I turn to look and see my mother standing there.

"Well, well, well, fatty needs her clothes specially made now?"

"Fuck you!" I say, louder than I planned.

Everyone comes out from the back and Mel storms over.

"Get the hell out of here. NOW!" Mel shouts.

"Still a foul-mouthed bitch.' my mother says.

Helen walks over and addresses my mother. "Ma'am, these ladies have an appointment, so I'll kindly ask you to remove yourself from the premises."

"Whatever. Oink, oink, piggy." she says then turns on her heel and walks out.

I feel a tear slide down my cheek and immediately feel like a fool.

"I'm so sorry, sweetie. How long's it been since you've seen her?" Mel asks.

"They showed up at the dog park when Damien and I were there yesterday. Damien ended up decking my father. It would have been worse, but Judd was driving by and ran in to stop him."

"That was your mother?" Alex says in disbelief.

"Afraid so."

Helen walks over and gives me a big hug, something my mother has never done. Alex and Mel join her, and I start to feel better. Helen takes them in the back so they can try their dresses on now that the interruption is over. A few minutes later, they come out from the back. They're both wearing floor length chiffon dresses with short sleeves and a leg slit. The shade of plum is exactly what I had in mind.

"Those are perfect, my beauties!" I exclaim.

Alex looks over at Helen and says, "Wrap up all three."

Mel and Alex follow Helen so they can change. Helen returns a few minutes later with three garment bags. "Where shall I have these delivered?" Helen asks.

"My house, please." Alex says. She hands Helen her credit card.

"What are you doing?" I ask Alex.

"The dresses are my treat, part of my wedding gift."

"You don't need to do that!" I say.

"I want to."

"Thank you."

Once Alex finishes up with Helen, we all thank her and head out to the car. Alex drives us to her friend's restaurant, Garden of Eden, for lunch. Eden and her husband Johnny are behind the counter when we walk in. Johnny is also the twin brother of Alex's best friend Hannah. Alex told me they were separated when they were young after their parents divorced and didn't find out about each other until recently. Their story sounds like something out of a book.

Eden walks over and hugs Alex. She walks our group to a table near the window and hands us each a menu. We all order iced teas. Eden brings them over and takes our orders. While we're waiting, Mel goes to the ladies room and Alex walks up to the counter to chat with Eden and Johnny, leaving me at the table. Mel returns a few minutes later. When lunch is ready, Alex helps Eden carry the plates to our table. After we eat a delicious lunch and share a dessert, we head out. Alex again insists on paying.

"I feel so spoiled." I say.

"You're the bride-to-be, you deserve to be spoiled!" Alex says.

"Now for our last stop, mani/pedis." Mel jokes.

We get to the salon, and when we walk inside, Lizzie, Hannah, and Eden are waiting for us.

"We decided to expand the party," Alex says. "We have the salon to ourselves."

We each take a seat in one of the salon chairs. The staff brings us each a mimosa and a small plate of fruit and cheese. One of the employees turns on music and tunes into our favorite 80s hair metal. I will never stop drooling over those sexy men in tight spandex and leather. Damien's in trouble when his horny woman gets home later.

I sit back for my day of pampering. This is exactly what I needed. I'm grateful this amazing group of women exist and accepted Mel and I. She was the only female friend I had growing up, so I didn't realize what I'd been missing out on. Not only did we get manis and pedis, we also got facials, as well as our hair and makeup done. When we were done, we all walked up front. We all hug goodbye. Hannah, Lizzie, and Eden get in Hannah's car and head home. Alex drops Mel off first then takes me home, where I see Dean and Damien sitting on the porch.

When we get out of the car and walk up, both of them stand and their jaws drop.

Dean runs off the porch and says, "We need to go home. Now!" They jump in Alex's car and race out of our driveway.

Damien turns to me and says, "Get your ass in that bedroom!"

I need to get pampered more often!

Chapter Seven

Damien

I wake up alone on Sunday morning. I wander down to the kitchen and see Lexi hard at work. Now that we have the basement setup, we're having everyone over to watch the Eagles game today. They deny it, but I think the girls just watch it to see the men in their tight uniform pants. I've noticed that Lexi becomes a different person when she watches sports. She loves yelling at the TV! She's especially fired up today since her Eagles are playing one of their biggest rivals, the Dallas Cowboys.

After we got the pool table, we went out and added the bar, some stools, a big screen TV and plenty of seating for our friends. Lexi's in heaven with the set up. She has yet to allow me any shenanigans on the pool table, but I get a feeling she's planning something. She takes a break from getting things ready for later to make me breakfast. I take care of the dogs and put the coffee on.

After we eat, I help her finish up then clean everything up. We go grab showers and get dressed. Lexi's in her favorite jeans and an Eagles jersey, and damn does she look sexy as hell! I grab her and pull her close, my hands firmly planted on that sweet ass of hers. I kiss her hard and feel her melt against me. Suddenly, I can't wait for everyone to go home and they're not even here yet. I might make her leave the jersey on when I fuck her later!

We head back downstairs. We take everything that we can down to the basement and get things setup. We head back up so she can figure out what she wants to heat up when. We take the dogs for a long walk before everyone comes then she gets to work. I go down to the basement and get all the chafing dishes ready so as she gets stuff cooked, we can take it down to keep it warm.

It's close to noon, so Lexi yells down for me to put the Fox pregame show on. Lexi loves Terry Bradshaw and that crew, so she watches that show religiously every Sunday. Not long after the show starts, everyone starts arriving. Lexi was happy when she invited Judd that he accepted and I'm betting Mel will be too. The guys are all carrying stuff when they come down, and now we have even more food. But with five always-hungry musicians and a cowboy, I suspect there won't be many leftovers.

The girls all come down together, helping Lexi carry the last few things. All six of them are dressed similarly in jeans and football jerseys. I look at the other guys and every one of them, myself included, can't peel our eyes away.

"I need to say something quick," Mikael says. "That right there," pointing at them, "are the six hottest women in the world."

The rest of us agree. I can't help but look at Judd and he will not take his eyes off Mel. I feel my resistance slipping and I think I need to help Lexi get them together. I shake off the thought when I hear Lexi tell everyone to help themselves to food. She's about to get up and make a plate when I stop her.

"You worked hard all morning. Let me get you some food." I say.

"Thanks, Damien, but I'm fine." I say.

"I insist. You sit and ogle those dudes in their tight pants while I grab you some food."

"Listen here! That's not why I watch football. Keep it up and I'll spike a ball off your head." she teases.

"Damn, girl, calm down." Mel teases as she walks by to get some food.

I look over and a smile threatens to creep onto Judd's face. I swear I see Mel shake her hips when she walks past. I walk over and hand Lexi her plate then lean in and whisper in her ear, "We need to get those two together."

She opens her mouth to react but I give her a look and she nods slightly. I know I'm going to regret this later. Halftime rolls around and the Eagles are down by seven, so alternate universe Lexi is sitting on the couch, arms across her chest, scowling. And, of course, I find it sexy as hell. It's a wonder we ever leave the bedroom. I look over at the pool table and my head fills with images of her naked body lying there waiting for me. Fuck, I need to focus on something else before my dick gives me away.

The second half of the game goes much better and the Eagles are trying a last ditch effort to pull out a victory. Lexi's on her feet and when the running back breaks free and scores with no time left on the clock, Lexi jumps up and down, her sexy tits bouncing. I start thinking of everything under the sun to keep from getting hard. Dean walks over to where I'm standing, a smirk on his face.

"That couch is gonna see some action after we leave." he says.

I give him the finger, but he's right. The minute the last of them leaves, that woman is gonna have my dick inside her. I can barely contain myself. I see Dean walk over to where Andy, Mikael, and Johnny are standing. They all turn and look at me, with amused looks on their faces. Dicks. About an hour after the game, everyone started getting ready to head out. When Lexi and the other girls started carrying food upstairs, the guys gave me shit.

"Do you think we'll even be out of the driveway?" Johnny asks.

"Did you see the way he was lookin' at her? Doubtful." Mikael says.

The guys kept up their ribbing, laughing their asses off. I hear a throat clear and the women are standing there watching us.

"I don't even want to know." Lexi says.

"You'll find out!" Dean says with a wink.

"I swear, that's all they think about..." Hannah teases.

"Oh and you don't, Mrs. Horny." Mikael says.

I see Lexi walk over to Mel when she sees the sad look on her face. Judd's isn't much different. He thanks me for having him then quickly leaves. I feel bad that we were carrying on in front of him. Mel leaves shortly after. We walk the rest of the group to their cars and watch until the last car is gone. I grab Lexi and pull her close.

"Get your ass back to that basement, woman."

"Something tells me I'm about to feel really good."

"Oh, fuck, yeah, woman."

I laugh as she practically runs for the door. When I get inside, I grab her and pull her close.

"Couch now!" I say.

"Excuse me, but I made all that delicious food."

"And?" I tease.

"You should be thanking me." she laughs.

"Then, your wish is my command, my love. What would you like to do first?"

"Dance. Will you put something slow on?"

I get up and turn the stereo on. I pull up the playlist of love songs that I made just for her when I first fell for her. I put it on shuffle and let my phone decide what to play. I walk back to the couch and hold my hand out. I walk us to the middle of the basement and pull her in tight. She rests her head on my chest.

"I love listening to your heart beat." she whispers.

"I love you, baby."

"I love you too."

After a couple of songs, I feel her hands slide under my shirt and rub my chest. She looks up at me and one look into those beautiful emerald eyes and I know what she wants. I raise my arms and my shirt hits the floor.

Before I get a chance to respond, her lips are on mine and her tongue's eagerly exploring my mouth. That's all it takes and I'm hard. Her hands move to my ass and she gives me a hard squeeze. I feel her hands move around my waist and unfasten my jeans. I kick my shoes off and step out of my jeans. She looks me up and down, her eyes stopping to gaze at the bulge threatening to tear a hole in my underwear. Without another word, she walks over to the couch.

She points down at my underwear. I remove them and watch as she licks her lips. She wags her finger at me, so I come over to where she's standing. She points down at her jeans. I pull them and her panties off. She locks eyes with me and starts to lift off her jersey but I stop her.

"Please leave it on. You look so damn sexy like that."

"Mmmm, my naughty man."

She bends over to take her sneakers and socks off and again, I stop her. "Baby, I want you just as you are now. I'm so fucking turned on. Get your ass on that couch."

She caresses my lips and points between her legs. I get down on the floor. She spreads her legs wide and puts them on my shoulders. I swipe my tongue up the entire length of her sweet pussy, stopping to suck on her clit. She moans as I feel her fingers in my hair. She tastes like no other woman and I can't get enough. Her body writhes, her hips rocking as I bring her closer to orgasm. Her body quakes as she succumbs to the pleasure. I take my tongue and lap up every last drop of her sweet honey.

"Stand up." she commands.

I stand up and she wraps her pretty mouth around my cock. She slides her head back and forth, sucking me hard and fast. Her fingers tease my balls. She removes her lips from my dick and sucks on my balls. Holy shit, this woman! She returns her mouth to my dick and fuck those lips feel so good.

I don't know how much more of this I can take. As if she read my mind, she sits back down. I open her legs and lift them. I slide my dick inside her pussy until it disappears. I fuck her hard, my balls slapping against that sexy ass. I match her with deep, hard thrusts until I feel her drench my cock. That's all it takes to send me over the edge and I come inside her hard. I collapse next to her on the couch, chest heaving. I never want to stop feeling like this. I take a hand and caress her cheek as our lips meet.

Her hand makes its way between my legs and starts stroking my cock until I'm hard again. It only took about 30 seconds of feeling that soft hand on me. She stands up and climbs onto my lap. She grabs my dick and lowers herself down on me. I need to see the rest of her, so I lift her jersey off and toss it aside. As she's bouncing on my dick, she slowly opens her bra and tosses it aside.

Her sexy breasts bounce in my face as she fucks me. I take turns sucking her breasts and teasing her nipples with my tongue, as my hands massage her sexy ass. She leans in and crushes her lips to mine. Her tongue finds mine and fuck, I love that feeling. She breaks the kiss a few minutes later.

"Fuck, I'm coming, baby!" she cries out.

For the second time, she squirts hard and soaks my dick. I fill her sweet pussy as I come hard. She collapses into me, her chest heaving against mine. My dick, still resting inside her, gets hard again.

"Baby, get on the couch and face the back. Now, hold on tight."

I slide inside her from behind. She's soaked from her orgasms and I slide in with ease. I reach a hand around and stroke her clit hard while I fuck her. It doesn't take long and we're both screaming as we come together.

"Holy shit, woman." I say.

"That was incredible," she says breathlessly. "I think we might need to shower now, though."

"I think you might be right."

We don't even bother getting dressed. We gather up our clothes and walk upstairs. As I'm following Lexi down the hall, I start laughing hysterically.

She stops and turns around. "And just what's so funny?"

I'm laughing so hard, all I can do is point. She looks down and starts laughing at herself. She's still wearing her socks and sneakers. We were so wrapped up in pleasuring each other, we never took notice until I was walking behind her.

"I must look like a jackass!" she says.

"Far from it. Truthfully, it's the sexiest thing I've ever seen."

By the time we reach the bedroom, I'm hard again. She notices and a wicked grin spreads across her beautiful face. She turns her back to me and bends down to remove her socks and shoes.

"Get your hot ass in the shower, now!" she commands.

We get into the shower stall and she puts a towel on the floor. She kneels on the towel and takes my entire length in her mouth. She runs her lips and tongue up and down my dick until I come in her mouth.

"Damn, woman."

She swallows every last drop as I turn on the shower. The hot water feels amazing running down my body while I watch my sexy woman wash her body and hair. She insists on washing me. We're both famished after our post-game party so we grab some leftovers from the fridge. We take the food upstairs and watch TV in bed.

After we're done eating, we lay down together. I watch her eyes start to droop. She's quickly asleep, so I pull the covers up. I watch her for a few minutes and start to feel my own eyes getting heavy. That's the last thing I remember until I'm awakened by Lexi screaming.

I shake her awake. "Baby, what's wrong?"

Chapter Eight

Lexi

"What do you mean what's wrong? Why are the dogs glued to me?" I ask.

"You started screaming in your sleep. You woke me up and the dogs came running."

All of a sudden, I remember why. "I had a nightmare, but it was silly." I say.

"Baby, tell me about it."

"My parents were calling me all those names from the other day, but this time, instead of defending me, you joined in. Even Maggie and Dave started talking and calling me names. Then everyone left me alone at the park."

I can't stop myself and my eyes spill over. Damien holds me close which helps.

"You, my love, are the most beautiful, most incredible woman I've ever known. You will never have to worry about that happening." Damien says.

"I love you."

"I love you too." Damien says. Suddenly, he laughs.

"What's so funny?"

"I'm trying to picture Dave and Maggie talking."

I can't help but laugh. "Thanks for making me feel better." I say.

"Anything for you. Now, how about we grab a shower and enjoy breakfast out back?"

"That sounds great." I say.

After we shower, we both get dressed and head to the kitchen. Damien gets Dave and Maggie their breakfast while I start cooking. While the dogs engage in their daily race to see who can empty their bowl first, Damien puts coffee on. He goes to the closet and grabs a hoodie for each of us. Now that fall is here, the mornings are nice and cool.

"I was thinking maybe we could get something to enclose the porch for the cold weather. That way we can still sit out back without freezing." Damien says.

"I love that idea. Maggie still loves to run and play, even in the cold, so this way, I won't freeze my ass off."

"That would be tragic. I love that hot little ass."

"Are you ever not horny?" I tease.

"Not since I met you, baby."

After I finish cooking, we eat and clean up. We're sitting out back enjoying another cup of coffee when I hear a car pull into the driveway. I look over and see Mel walking towards us. A few minutes later, Judd appears at the fence. He climbs over and joins us. That's all it takes for my wheels to start spinning.

"Can I get either of you coffee or something else to drink?" I ask.

"Coffee, please." Mel says.

"Same for me." Judd says.

"Damien, would you mind helping me?" I ask.

Damien follows me inside. Judd takes a seat at the table while Mel goes to play with the dogs. I grab two cups of coffee and put them on the counter. I grab the creamer and a sweetener selection and put them on a tray. I put the cups and the coffee pot onto the tray. I'm about to carry it outside when chaos erupts.

As if in slow motion, Mel bends down to pick up a tennis ball. Dave comes running full speed ahead and before anyone can react, she's on her ass. I see her lean forward, grabbing her ankle and wincing. We're about to run outside when I see Judd walk down and scoop Mel up in his arms. He carries her over to the table and sits her down in one of the chairs. The dreamy look on her face is unmistakable. She's falling for him.

Damien turns and looks at me, a huge smile on his face. "Dave the Matchmaker strikes again!" he jokes.

"I'm beginning to think you trained him to do this." I tease.

We carry the tray outside and lay it on the table. I look down at Dave and I swear that's a shit-eating grin I see on his furry face.

"I'm so sorry. Are you okay, Mel?" Damien asks.

"No worries. I just twisted my ankle when I went down."

"Dave can be a bit overzealous," I say. "I should know."

"He can, but he's such a handsome fella that all is forgiven. Besides, I had my knight in shining armor to help me." Mel says as she giggles like a schoolgirl.

Judd turns a bright shade of red, which makes him even more handsome. If these two knuckleheads don't figure out soon that they belong together, I'm going to take it up a notch. I hope that Dave's antics today laid the groundwork.

Damien and I sit down at the table and I pour four cups of coffee. As we're sitting there drinking, an idea pops into my head.

"What do you all think about a Halloween costume party at the club?" I ask.

"I love costume parties!" Mel says.

"I was thinking maybe having a theme, like famous movie and TV couples or something." I add.

"Oh, I love that," Mel says. "I'm just bummed I won't be able to go."

"Why not?" Judd asks.

"I can't go alone." Mel says, a sad look in her eyes.

"Well, ma'am, I'd be honored if you'd allow me to escort you. As friends of course, but we could still pick out a couple to dress as." Judd says.

"Are you sure? I'd hate to put you out." Mel responds.

"It sounds like fun, so I'd love for you to accompany me."

"Well, then, I accept." Mel says.

The biggest smile I've ever seen flashes on Judd's face but quickly disappears. The usual pain reappears in his eyes. I look over at Damien, who has that familiar naughty look in his eye.

"Okay, out with it." I say to Damien.

"Can we please be Danny and Sandy from Grease?" Damien asks.

"Really?" I ask. "You want me to be a goody-goody?" I ask.

"No silly. I want Sandy from that part at the end. I need to see you in the tight black pants and shirt. And please god, the red heels!" Damien says.

"That makes more sense," I say. "I thought you wanted me to be pure Sandy."

"No way in hell you could pull that off.," Damien laughs.

"What do you mean by that? I'm as innocent as they come!" I say, batting my eyelashes at him.

Mel laughs so hard that she snorts. And not a quiet snort, she lets out the loudest snort I've ever heard.

"Oh my god, I'm so sorry." she says, her cheeks beet red.

"I thought it was cute." Judd says.

Damien's jaw drops. That's the first we've ever heard him say anything like that. Mel giggles again. I don't say anything out loud but I'm screaming at them inside my head. I know Damien's planning to ask Judd to be his best man, so who knows, maybe something will happen at our wedding. I also know Mel needs to shed some of her demons first, aka her bitch of a younger sister. You could write an entire full-length novel about the shit she's done to my best friend.

Damien hears the dogs start barking so he goes down to throw the ball for them. Judd joins him, leaving Mel and I alone. I look at her and her eyes are locked on Judd's ass. I love Damien, but damn, I can still admire a hot ass, and Judd's is one of the hottest I've ever seen.

"Oh my god, girl!" I exclaim.

"What?" Mel says.

"Don't even play that. You know you want that man."

"It doesn't matter what I want. It'll never happen."

"And why's that?"

"My sister' right. I'm damaged goods and no man will ever want me."

"Forgive me for saying this, but fuck that bitch. You're the most amazing woman I've ever known. You befriended me when nobody else would. You're beautiful, kind, generous, intelligent, successful, and so much more. Any man would be lucky to have you."

"Thanks, Lex. It just gets so hard sometimes. But I don't need to tell you that, after what your parents put you through."

"I know one thing, girl. We're going to pick the sexiest couple ever for yours and Judd's costume. I want to find something that'll make that man drool. And hey, while we're on that topic, I need your help with something."

"Of course, what?"

I fill Mel on a plan I have for Damien. She's practically panting by the time I'm done.

"I know just the dress. Is tomorrow okay, just so I can give my ankle a chance to rest?"

"Of course, and if you need longer, I can wait."

"No way in hell would I make you wait for that, girl!"

We both laugh so loud that Damien and Judd stop dead in their tracks and just stare at us.

Chapter Nine

Damien

"Do we want to know what that's about?" Judd asks me .

"Nope!" Lexi and Mel are sitting at the table. Their heads are together and they're in hysterics, which likely means they're up to no good.

The dogs have worn themselves out and no longer run after the ball. They curl up in a sunny spot in the corner of the yard, so Judd and I head back to the table. Just as we arrive, Mel looks down at her watch.

"I need to head out. I had the morning off, but I have a meeting this afternoon, so I need to go prepare." Mel says.

She tries to stand and winces in pain. "Shit, I twisted it a little worse than I thought."

"Allow me to help you to your car." Judd says.

Before Mel can answer, he carries her to her car, Lexi and I in tow. Lexi opens the door so Judd can set her down inside.

"Are you going to be okay when you get to work?" Lexi asks.

"All good. Thank you, Judd, for the assistance." Mel says, as she lowers her eyes and gives him a flirty look.

He tips his hat and says, "My pleasure, ma'am."

After Mel pulls out of the driveway, Judd heads back to his ranch. I grab Lexi's hand as we walk back to the patio. The dogs are sound asleep in the grass so we sit down at the table. One look at Lexi's face and I know what it's time to discuss.

"Oh my god, can you believe what we just witnessed?" Lexi exclaims.

"I know. I tried to fight you on this, but damn if those two don't belong together." I say.

"Right. Even Dave can see it! Now we need to get them to. I'm hoping the Halloween party will take them another step closer."

"Same. We just need to not interfere too much."

"I know. It needs to happen naturally. It's just that it makes me sad to see her so down. Him too. I still feel like he's buried some pretty deep wounds."

"Me too. Maybe having a woman to love is what he needs to move past some of it."

"And Mel's been through her share of hell. She carries herself well, but deep down, there's a lot of pain. There's things I've never told you, and can't because it's hers to tell, but trust me, it's amazing she's the person she is."

"Both of you are obviously who you are despite your family."

"Truth right there. You've been key in helping me discover the woman that was hiding inside a very broken shell. I'll never truly be able to thank you."

"Like hell you won't. Just the fact that you're in my arms every night is thank you enough. Don't forget, you helped me too, babe. Come with me for a minute."

I help her up and walk her down to the pond. I grab my phone out of my pocket and turn on Is This Love by Whitesnake. I pull her close and we start dancing as the leaves from the oak tree drop around us. This woman just feels like home to me and I cannot wait until New Year's Eve when she becomes my wife. She looks up at me and leans her head toward mine. My lips meet hers and she opens for me. I slide my tongue into her mouth. She intertwines her tongue with mine. I can feel my dick starting to get hard - big shock, I know - and I need to get her inside now.

We bring the dogs inside and beeline to the bedroom. After a very passionate lovemaking session, we take a long nap. I wake up and my stomach is growling. A wicked idea makes its way into my brain, due in large part to the beautiful naked woman lying next to me. I wake her with a gentle kiss to those sexy lips, still swollen from my dick.

"Hi, sleepyhead." I say.

"Mmmm, thanks to that sexy cock." she says.

"I have an idea. Tell me what you think."

"Okay."

"Let's pack a picnic and eat on the dock at the park."

"That sounds perfect!"

After we shower and get dressed, we head downstairs. I get our dinner ready while Lexi takes care of the dogs. We take them for a quick walk then head out ourselves. I carry the food and drinks and Lexi carries the blankets. It's been getting chillier at night now that October's here, but I have a feeling she'll be plenty warm later.

This dock has seen its share of action, especially from our group of friends. I'm planning to add some when I get my woman naked later. I take one of the blankets from her and lay it down on the doc.

"Have a seat, my love." I say.

She takes a seat and smiles up at me. My heart swells, and well, so does something else! I open the basket and spread out the food. I pour us each a glass of wine. As we sit and eat, the sun starts to set, replaced by an almost-full moon. I watch Lexi as she gazes out at the lake.

"The colors look so beautiful reflecting off the water. It looks like everything's dancing."

"Speaking of dancing, would you give me the honor of a dance?"

"I'd love to!"

I help her up and pull her in close. Instead of turning music on, I quietly sing into her ear. She melts into me, lifts her head and kisses me hard. We sway together under the stars, kissing each other passionately.

"I wanna make love right here on the dock." she whispers.

"Baby, that's exactly why I brought you here tonight." I say.

Without a word, she strips and lays down on the blanket. I quickly remove my clothes and lay next to her. I pull her in close and kiss her hard. I run my hand down her side until I reach her thigh. I slide my hand over and tease her pussy with my fingers. She moans into my mouth as I slip a couple of fingers inside her. I slide my fingers in out, feeling her get wetter and wetter. I slide my fingers out and focus on her clit. She grinds against me, as I feel her hand stroke my dick.

"Baby, that feels so good." I say.

"Mmm, Damien." she moans.

I position myself between her legs and slide my dick inside her. I feel her hands grab my ass and pull me closer. Slowly, I slide in and out of her glorious body. She lightly rakes her nails up and down my back as we move together. The cool autumn air feels refreshing against the heat of our bodies. I start nearing my climax so I stop moving.

"Please don't stop," Lexi moans.

"Baby, I want this night to last."

"Oh, Damien."

We experience several orgasms together before we're both spent. I lie down next to her and pull the other blanket on top of us. I'm overwhelmed by the feeling of bliss I experience holding her like this. I look up at the sky and see a shooting star.

"Baby, look. Make a wish quick," I say.

She looks up, a smile on her face.

"What did you wish for?" I ask.

"Since we already have the love we both desired, I wished for Judd and Mel to find the same thing."

I kiss her forehead. "I love you, Lexi."

"I love you so much, Damien."

We continue lying on the dock in each other's arms until we hear rustling in the grass nearby. We quickly pull on our clothes. Two figures appear from the woods, laughing. I know those voices all too well, so I clear my throat and hear them gasp. Lexi loses it and starts laughing hysterically as Dean and Alex appear on the dock.

"Well, well, well, what do we have here?" I tease them.

"Umm, just a late night stroll." Dean says.

"So, that's what the kids are calling it these days." I joke.

"Hey, what about you two?" Dean says.

"Just enjoying some dinner." I say.

"Oh, is that so? I can only imagine what it was you ate, dude." Dean says.

"Guess we should all get out of here before we get caught." Lexi says.

"I'm with Lexi." Alex says.

The four of us walk out together. We reach the parking lot just as another car pulls in.

"Well, apparently, something's in the air tonight!" Lexi says.

We all laugh when we see Mikael and Hannah get out of their car with a couple of blankets. After a few minutes of everyone teasing each other, Mikael and Hannah head toward the dock. Alex and Dean head home, and we do the same.

The next morning, after we finish breakfast, we take the dogs out back. Judd takes a break from his work and stops over. A little while later, Lexi gets up.

"I'm off to pick up Mel. Be home later." she says then heads to the garage. A few minutes later, I hear her pull out.

"The ladies are going shopping." I say to Judd.

"How's Mel's ankle?"

"Better. Lexi called her last night and she was able to walk without any pain."

"I'm glad."

"I've been wanting to ask you something..." I say.

"Shoot."

"Would you consider being best man at Lexi's and my wedding?"

"I'd be honored."

"Great. Thanks, man. You'll be walking with Mel. Speaking of Mel, level with me, dude."

"What do you mean?"

"You got a thing for her, don't ya?"

A smile briefly appears on his face, but quickly fades. "I can't."

"Why not?"

"I need to get back to work."

"Okay." An awkward silence fills the air. "I'll let you know when I schedule the tux fitting."

"Cool." Judd says then walks back to his ranch.

I hope Lexi's having better luck with Mel.

Chapter Ten

Lexi

I pull into Mel's driveway and see that she's waiting on her porch for me. She gets in and we head for the mall.

"Okay, woman, we need to talk." I say.

"About?" Mel asks.

"Oh like you don't know. A certain cowboy that curls your toes."

"I'm not interested in Judd."

"Oh, so that wasn't you getting all giggly with him? I know you way better than that."

"Okay, yeah, so what. I think he's great, but you know it can never happen."

"You deserve to be with someone. And newsflash, I think he likes you too!"

"It doesn't matter. My sister's right. I'm damaged and useless to men."

"Stop that. I know better than anyone how you feel, but not every man is looking for that. Damien wasn't."

"I don't want to talk about this anymore. Let's go get you some sex clothes."

"Thanks for making it sound creepy, you bitch!"

"My pleasure! Actually, it'll be your pleasure."

"This is why I love you."

"Right back at ya."

I park outside one of the big department stores. Mel drags me inside and right to wear the dresses are. Truth is, I hate this shit. I would rather be in jeans and a t-shirt or, when I'm with Damien, naked. But I have a plan and the black dress I hope to find is key. She picks a bunch of stuff off a rack and pushes me toward the dressing room. I put on the first dress she hands me and make her come in. I'm way too mortified to let anyone else see me.

"Oh my god, woman. Damien's going to be panting like a puppy when he sees you. This is definitely the one. Oh, and I highly recommend you go commando."

"I was planning to."

After I change back into my clothes, I pay for the dress. We head out into the mall and find the Halloween store so we can go costume shopping. I luck out and find a replica of Sandy's outfit in Grease. Mel finds a very sexy witch costume. I have a feeling a certain cowboy might get ridden that night! We pay for our stuff and head back to the department store.

All of a sudden, I hear a female voice behind us say, "Oh, look, someone let the pigs out of their pen."

I turn around and see Mel's younger sister, Trish, standing behind us. "Seriously, that's all you got?" I ask.

"Plenty more where that came from if you can take it." Trish says.

"If it makes you feel better about your pathetic existence, feel free to keep insulting me." I say.

"Nothing to add, loser?" Trish says to Mel.

All of a sudden, Trish's eyes go wide and her mouth drops open. "Shit, they're hot. You know, the type of men neither of you would ever get with."

"Actually, you couldn't be more wrong." I feel Damien's arm circle my waist. "I don't believe we've had the pleasure. Damien St. James, future husband of this beauty." he says as he tousles my hair.

I see Judd walk over and lightly lay a hand on Mel's arm. "Judd Walker, ma'am."

Trish's face turns bright red as a scowl appears on her face. Without a word, she turns on her heel and stomps away. I look at Mel just as a couple of tears spill over. She looks down at her feet then walks over to a bench and sits down.

"What are you guys doing here?" I ask.

"We decided we wanted to treat two pretty ladies to lunch." Damien says and puts his arm out. I link my arm through his. Judd walks over to Mel and puts out his hand, which she accepts. He links her arm through his and the four of us walk down to the food court. Mel and I sit down at a table while the guys go order.

"Tell me again, girl, how you two don't belong together." I say to Mel while we're waiting.

"I know you mean well, but please, just drop it." she says.

I nod, but don't say anything. We both just sit quietly until the guys return with a couple of trays. Judd hands Mel her lunch and that rare smile crosses his face. I see her hand brush his and the dreamiest look appears on her face. Damien and I just look at each other, but don't say anything. He hands me a slice of pizza and a soda. After lunch the guys walk with us until they reach the entrance where they parked. Mel and I walk back to the department store where we parked.

"I forgot something I need. Do you mind if we're here a little longer?" I ask.

"Anything I can help with?" Mel asks.

"Actually, yeah. Unless it's sneakers, I know nothing about buying shoes."

"Okay, tell me what you're thinking and I'll find the right shoe."

"First, I need something that looks similar to what Sandy wears at the end of Grease. And I also need something super-sexy to go with the black dress."

Mel takes my hand and nearly rips my arm off dragging me to the shoe section. She finds the perfect "Sandy" shoe first. Then she grabs a pair of black stilettos.

"There's no way in hell I could walk in those!" I say.

"You don't need to. Trust me, these are strictly "fuck me now" shoes. Just carry them with you and put them on when you get in position. And be prepared for Damien to make you leave them on when you fuck."

"Oh my god, Mel!"

"You mark my words. And woman, I better get details."

"But, of course!"

After I pay for my shoes, we walk to the parking lot and head to Mel's house.

"I'm sorry I snapped at you earlier. I was just upset after seeing Trish."

"I shouldn't have pushed. I'm sorry too."

"Can I tell you a secret?"

"Of course."

"I think I may have feelings for Judd. But, I just can't act on it. So, just promise me you won't say anything."

"I promise."

I drop her off, make one quick stop, then head home. Now I just need to put the final phase of my plan in action. Damien's in for the night of his life! I leave my bags in the car for now. I can hear the dogs in the backyard so I walk out and see Damien playing with them. I walk over to Damien and give him a hard smack on his sexy ass. I catch a whiff of his shower gel and I almost melt.

"Damn, woman." Damien says.

"I can't resist that sexy ass." I say.

I grab him and plant a kiss on his lips that makes my intentions quite clear. He groans into my mouth. When he tries to pull me into the house, I stop him. "All in due time," I say, lowering my eyes. "For now, though, could you pick us up some Chinese food? I'm starving and don't feel like waiting for delivery."

"After what you just did, you got it!"

We walk inside to order then Damien heads out. I run upstairs, grab a quick shower throw a robe on, and grab my bags out of my car. I put the dress on, and as Mel said, showcase "the girls." I put the stilettos on the pool table until I have everything else ready. I leave a brand new pair of lace panties in the kitchen with a note attached. The items I purchased on the way home from Mel's sit in a bag.

I hear Damien pull in the driveway, so I get up onto the pool table and put the shoes on. I can hear him walking around upstairs. When I hear the basement door open and close, I grab the remote for the stereo and turn on the special playlist I made for tonight. I watch as he walks down the steps, stumbling over the last two when he sees me.

"Holy fucking shit, woman!"

Chapter Eleven

Damien

All I can do is stand there, gaping at the vision before me. Getting home and seeing those lace panties was enough to make me go weak in the knees. But, then I read the note.

Dearest Sexy Rockstar,

Get that hot ass down to the basement! NOW!

I'm going to give you a night you'll NEVER forget!

Love,

Your Horny as Hell Fiancee

I'm frozen in place. She's lying on her side on the pool table, which is now covered in a red velvet blanket, in the sexiest fucking pose I've ever seen. Her delicious breasts spill out of her dress and all I can think about is wrapping my mouth around them. Then I see the shoes. And boom, my erection strains against my jeans. I'm rendered completely speechless, and still, all I can do is stand here gawking at my sexy woman.

"Earth to sexy rockstar," she teases. "See something you like?"

"Oh, fuck yeah. Something I love and something I want."

"Then, what are you waiting for? Get that hot ass over here. NOW!"

I walk over to the pool table and stand in front of her. She swings her legs over and opens them just enough for me to see she's not wearing panties. I start sweating just thinking about being inside her. She lifts my shirt over my head and rakes her nails down my chest. A wicked smile unlike any I've seen from her yet spreads across her gorgeous face. She grabs the bag sitting next to her.

"Turn around and close your eyes. No peeking, or you won't get to play."

I do as I'm told. I feel her take one of my arms behind my back. I feel something furry tease my wrist. She repeats the same on my other wrist. My hands are now cuffed behind my back.

"Open your eyes and turn around."

I'm completely at her mercy and fuck am I turned on. She reaches into the bag again and pulls out a bottle. Flavored massage oil! She squeezes some into her hands and rubs it on my chest. The sweet scent of pineapple fills the room. She rubs her hands all over my chest and my neck. She pulls me closer and leans her head toward me.

She runs her tongue all over my neck, licking and sucking. She drags her tongue all over my chest and my knees go weak. She turns me around and rubs oil on my shoulders and back. After another round of licking me, she tells me to face her. I love her being so dominant. And damn, so does my dick.

She reaches down and removes my belt, tossing it aside. She opens my jeans and they fall to the floor. She grabs the waistband on my underwear and slides them down, finally freeing my dick.

"Mmmm, I want a taste of that, baby." she purrs. She grabs a key and removes the handcuffs. "Get the rest of your clothes off and get up on this table."

I kick my clothes aside and climb up on the table. I reach out to touch her, but she lightly smacks my hand.

"Behave or the cuffs go back on," she says. "Now get on your back."

Lexi grabs another bottle out of the bag.

"What's that?" I ask.

"Oral sex gel." she says.

"Oh..." is all I manage to say before my breath catches in my throat. How can this be that same woman who was so shy that she wouldn't even look at me that night at the club? But, damn, I'm sure as hell glad it is. I have a sneaking suspicion this woman was always in there somewhere!

I watch as she squeezes some of the gel onto her hand. She runs her hand up and down my cock then rubs some on my balls. She gets on all fours, giving me full view of those luscious breasts. She teases my balls with her tongue and I groan. She moves her head slightly and takes my entire length into her mouth without even the slightest gag. She makes eye contact with me as she sucks my dick until I can't control myself. I fill her pretty mouth then watch as she swallows me down.

Seeing her in that dress gets me hard again. I watch her lower the straps, freeing her sexy breasts. She crawls up my body and squeezes them around dick. My jaw drops as I watch her.

"Woman." is the only word I can remember right now. She doesn't stop until I cover her chest with my seed. She grabs a towel out of the bag and cleans her breasts.

"Now that I've pleasured you, it's my turn." she says. She sits up and swings her legs over the side of the table. She lifts her sexy ass off the table and lets the dress fall to the floor. She reaches down to take one of her shoes off.

"Please, baby, for the love of all that is holy, leave those on." I say as drool runs down my chin.

"My, my, you are such a dirty man," she teases. "Now, you will do as I say. Unless, of course, you have a problem with that."

"I love when you tell me what to do. The dirtier, the better."

"I want you to give me the most sensual massage I've ever felt." she says as she hands me the bottle of oil.

I jump off the table and watch as she flips onto her stomach. I put some oil on my hands and start with her shoulders. I work my way down her back until it's covered in oil. She moans softly as I massage her. Now it's time for that sexy ass. Her moans get louder as I knead those sexy cheeks. I run my hands down the back of both legs until the entire back of her body is slick.

"Mmm, Damien." she moans as she lies on her back.

This time, I work my way up from her legs to her sexy neck. She's an absolute goddess lying there naked. Well, except for those hotter than hell shoes. She picks up the bottle of gel and waves it at me. Fuck, I can't wait to taste her sweet juices. I put some gel on my fingers and rub her pussy. Damn, she's so fucking wet.

I give her one slow swipe with my tongue. The gel tastes like cotton candy. I lower my mouth and cover her entire pussy. I suck and lick her as she writhes beneath me. I feel her body quake as she cries out. I rub a little more gel on and continue my oral assault on that hot pussy. Her cries turn to screams as she rides wave after wave of ecstasy. She tastes so fucking sweet that I don't want to stop. That is, until I hear my favorite words come out of her pretty lips.

"Damien, I want your cock inside me. NOW! There's one more thing in the bag."

I pull a wedge pillow out of the bag. She lifts her ass so I can slide it under her. Fuck, she looks so hot like that. The pillow has her at the perfect angle. She spreads her legs as wide as she can and all I can do is stare at her pussy.

"What the hell are you waiting for? I WANT that dick inside me NOW!" she commands.

Damn, I love this side of her. I climb back up on the table. Our skin is still slick from the massage oil, allowing me to easily slide up her sexy body. I take her arms and lift them over her head. I slide my dick inside her as slowly as possible. I want to savor how it feels when I'm inside her. She wraps her legs around me and I can feel those sexy shoes on my naked ass.

"Keep those arms stretched over your head, so I can watch those sexy breasts bounce while I fuck you."

She does as she's told as she arches her back. I keep my slow pace until I hear her cry out, "Oh, Damien, fuck me hard. I can take any pounding you give my pussy."

I fuck her hard and fast, not taking my eyes of her amazing chest. I can't control myself and come inside her hard. I slide my dick out and stroke her clit with it until her body shakes with another powerful orgasm.

"On your back." she demands.

I toss the pillow aside and lay down. She straddles me, grabs my dick, and lowers her body, taking all of me inside her. She sits up straight and holy shit does she look incredible when she rides me. She rides me painfully slow, driving my dick wild. She ignores my pleas to speed up, so instead I savor every long, slow, deep stroke of her pussy.

"Oh fuck, Damien." she cries out as she squirts hard, completely soaking me. Still, she resumes that slow pace. I feel like a caged tiger.

"Oh god, woman, please fuck me hard. I crave you, baby." I growl. She lays down on top of me. I wrap my arms tight around her and she finishes me off and I empty inside her. She moves next to me. I look over at this incredible woman and a wicked idea enters my mind.

"Baby, I've never seen you look more beautiful than you do right now. Will you let me photograph you?"

Her jaw drops and she stares at me, but she doesn't say a word. I hope I didn't go too far.

Chapter Twelve

Lexi

What did he just ask me? I shock myself when I get turned on by the thought of it.

"If you're not sure, it's okay. This has to be something you are one hundred percent comfortable with." Damien says.

"I want to." she whispers.

"Are you sure? Please, I need you not to be afraid to say no."

"I can't believe I'm saying this, but I really want to. I'm kinda turned on by the thought of it."

"How about on the couch?"

"Okay. Just let me get my shoes off so I can walk over."

"No way, those sexy shoes are staying on."

Damien gets off the pool table, scoops me into his arms and carries me over to the couch. I kneel on the couch, facing the back and look back at him. He's standing there with his tongue hanging out.

"Grab the handcuffs." I say.

He grabs the cuffs and walks over to the couch. I put my arms behind my back and he snaps them on. He walks over where his camera bag is hanging and returns with his camera in hand.

"Now, turn your head and look back at me. Give the sexiest look you can." he says.

He snaps a couple of pictures and I find myself getting more turned on. I lay on my side on the couch and prop my head on my hand. A couple more camera snaps. I do a few more tame poses then decide to up the naughty. I sit up on the couch and open my legs wide. Damien just stares at me but doesn't take any photos.

"Well, what are you waiting for?" I ask.

"A-a-are you sure you want one like that?" he asks.

"Please, baby."

"Damn, woman!" He snaps a couple photos then turns the camera off and sits down next to me. I look over and see his dick standing at full attention. I stand up without breaking my ankles on the shoes and face him. I climb onto his lap and slide him inside me. He pulls me in close and we fuck hard and fast. We both come quickly. We just sit there holding each other, his dick resting inside me.

"I don't even know what to say about tonight." Damien says to me.

"Did you enjoy yourself?" I ask.

"So fuckin' much. You're incredible. And so beautiful." he says.

"I don't know about the beautiful part..." I say.

"Well, I do. Sit next to me, I want to show you."

He grabs the camera and turns it on. He brings up the pictures he took. I'm afraid to look so I close my eyes.

"Baby, please open your eyes."

"Who's that?" I ask in disbelief.

"That's you. The sexy, stunning, amazing woman who completely stole my heart."

After so many years of put-downs and everything else, I realize that I had a very skewed image of myself. Seeing these pictures makes me realize just how wrong I've been. I can't stop a smile from spreading across my face.

"Let me see the rest." I whisper.

Damien scrolls through the rest of the pictures and they actually look good. He gets to that last one and I feel my breath catch in my throat. I just stare at myself. I'm sitting there completely naked, legs open, my pussy on full display. I'm leaning forward, elbows on my knees, my lips in a full pout. I can't believe the sentence that comes out of my mouth.

"I look sexy." I whisper.

"No whispering that. Shout it out loud."

"I look sexy."

"Louder. Scream it, woman."

"I LOOK SEXY!" I shout.

"Now, tell me how you feel." Damien says.

"Free."

He stands up, scoops me off the couch and lays me down on the pool table. Without a word, he's on top of me and his hard-again dick slides inside me. Slowly, sensually, we make love one last time. We're lying together afterwards when my stomach growls. I forgot all about dinner until that moment.

"How about we go heat up some of the food? I'm famished." I say.

"Me too."

I take the shoes off and climb off the pool table. I put my robe on and gather the dress and shoes. Damien pulls just his pants on and grabs the rest of his clothes. I put all our fun toys in a bag and grab the blanket off the pool table. We head up to the kitchen and make a couple plates of food. After the microwave does its thing, we head into the living room to eat. After we're done, I carry the plates to the kitchen and put them in the sink. Damien follows me and starts fiddling with the sash of my robe.

"Mmm, baby, I can't stop thinking how you're naked under that robe."

"And very, very wet."

He lifts me onto the counter and opens my robe.

"So beautiful." he says as he buries a couple of fingers inside me.

"Mmm, feels so good."

How I have anything left to give is beyond me, but next thing I know, I'm coming hard around his fingers. He lifts me off the counter and lays me down on the living room couch. Again, he's on top of me and inside me. He quickly fills me. Our bodies are covered in a delicious combination of sweat, massage oil and a couple other fun fluids.

"I need a shower." I say.

"Me too."

We take a long, steamy shower together and throw on some sweats. After we feed the dogs, we take them out back. The sun's going down much earlier now and the air gets chilly at night. Damien builds a fire in our fire pit. We sit there while the dogs run and play. My body still tingles from one of the hottest days I've ever had. When the dogs are done playing, Damien puts the fire out, at least the one in the fire pit, and we head back inside. We watch a movie then head off to bed.

Damien kisses me goodnight and whispers, "Thank you for a night I'll never forget."

"My pleasure."

The next morning, we finish up breakfast and take the dogs for a quick walk.

"I'll be meeting the guys in about an hour for our tux fitting," Damien says. "I'm taking them all out to lunch afterwards."

"Have fun! I'll be heading down the club to do some work then I need to stop at Hannah's shop and grab some stuff for the kiddos."

"Don't we sound like an old married couple!" he jokes.

I laugh. Truthfully, though, I love the idea of being his wife and spending the rest of our lives together. We both shower and get ready to head out. After I'm done at the club, I swing by Hannah's shop and grab two big bags of dog food and some treats for Maggie and Dave. Ever the gentleman, Mikael carries them out to my car. I give him and Hannah a hug goodbye then run over to Eden's to grab lunch.

After I get everything inside, I grab my lunch and my Kindle and take the dogs out back. I love being with Damien, but I also enjoy some alone time. After I eat, I open my Kindle and pull up one of the many romance novels waiting for me. I finish the book in one sitting, my brain now filled with some naughty new things to do to my sexy rockstar! He better be well-rested later!

Chapter Thirteen

Damien

I drive over to Shooting Star Ranch to pick up Judd. The other guys are meeting us at the Men's Warehouse.

"Hey man, thanks for doing this." I say when Judd gets in.

"I'm honored you asked," Judd replies. "Hey, can I ask you somethin'?"

"Shoot."

"Why isn't Mel with anyone?"

"I honestly don't know, man. Interested in her?"

"Just curious."

I have a feeling it's more than that, but I don't want to push. We ride the rest of the way in silence. I see the rest of the guys pulling up in Johnny's car as I'm parking. We all meet out front and walk in together.

"My name is Derek. How may I help you, gentlemen?"

"I'm Damien St. James. I have an appointment for a tux fitting."

"Right this way, sir."

We follow Derek over and notice a couple of female employees staring. Judd tips his hat to them, causing them to giggle and hurry off.

Derek takes everyone's measurements. I leave a deposit and contact information and we head outside. A few minutes later, a limo pulls up, followed by Hannah. I look and see Eden and Lexi with her. The ladies walk over and join us.

"What are you doing here?" I tease.

"Eden and I are here to take yours and Johnny's cars home," Lexi answers. "Have fun today."

Johnny and I hand our keys to our women and get in the limo.

"I thought we were just going to lunch." I say.

"Surprise! Welcome to your overnight bachelor party!" Dean says. "We arranged it with Lexi."

"Thanks, guys. Where we headed?"

"Atlantic City. We're staying in a suite overnight. The ladies will all be at your house for a girls sleepover." Mikael says.

I lean over and say to Judd, "Are you sure you're okay with this?"

"Yes, of course, I trust Lexi to take care of things until we get back tomorrow. This trip will do me some good." Judd says.

I sit and relax, watching the scenery as we go. My mind goes back to yesterday and the mind-blowing sex I had with my woman. Most of all, though, I can't stop thinking about the pictures. Fuck, that woman is stunning. Dean looks at me and starts laughing.

"What, man?" I ask.

"Thinking about Lexi, I see." He says.

"Whatcha mean?"

"Dude, that look on your face. Guessing she played with your dick last night?"

"I'll never tell."

The other guys egg Dean on as he keeps giving me shit. I know I would achieve legendary status if they knew about the pictures, but I would never betray Lexi like that. I'm grateful, though, that I used a camera and not my phone. We arrive a couple hours later, and the limo takes us to the VIP entrance. A bellhop meets us and puts our bags on a cart. After we check in, we head up to the suite to shower and change.

We head down to the casino, and heads, mostly female, turn and ogle us. If they only knew we were all spoken for already. Not one woman I've seen even comes close to my Lexi. We stop at a Blackjack table and play a few hands then head off to the Hard Rock Cafe for dinner. I definitely need to bring Lexi here sometime!

We order a couple of pitchers of beer for the table. We all look at the menu while we wait. Our waitress brings the beer and six glasses then takes our food order. We order a bunch of appetizers and burgers all around. Our overly-flirty waitress jokes about us ordering manly food as she bats her eyelashes.

After we finish our food and a few more pitchers of beer, the guys split the check, not letting me pay anything. We head back to the casino floor. Dean steers us toward the high roller area. We go inside and Dean walks over to the cashier area. A couple minutes later, one of the pit bosses takes us to a private room. On one side of the room is a poker table with six chairs and six stacks of chips.

On the other side is a regular table also with six chairs. A waitress brings in several pitchers of beer and glasses. She pours us each a glass and we sit down. A little while later, a woman comes in who I assume is our poker dealer. I was wrong! She puts a chair out and motions me over. I hear music and she starts dancing.

As she dances, clothes start coming off until she's in just a bra and panties. The guys are all cheering me on, but I feel these strange pangs. What the fuck? Holy shit, guilt. I must really love that woman! But, I know Lexi and I know she trusts me or she wouldn't have helped arrange this so I sit back and enjoy the show. When she's done, she says, "If you want more personal attention, that can be arranged."

"Thank you, but I'll pass." I say.

"Your bride-to-be is one lucky woman."

"I'm the lucky one." I say.

She leaves her card, congratulates me on my upcoming wedding and heads out. Our waitress brings us more pitchers of beer and some snacks. A dealer sits down at our poker table so we all take a seat and start with Texas Hold 'Em. Since we're just playing for fun, we decide to play an elimination tournament. As the evening progresses, Judd seems to relax more and it turns out, he's not that different from the rest of us.

We finally get down to two players, Judd and Andy. They seem pretty evenly matched skill-wise, as well as chip count. Judd has a slight edge, and puts Andy all-in. Andy flips over pocket queens, and makes a full house with the queen and two tens on the table. Unfortunately, he couldn't have picked a worst time, as Judd flips over pocket tens, giving him four-of-a-kind and the win.

"Damn, man, didn't know you played," I say. "Lexi does too."

"Maybe we need a tournament with all of us when we get home." Dean says.

We play a couple more tournaments and Judd wins them all. I can't wait to see him against Lexi. Around two in the morning, the pit boss comes in and lets us know they need to close down the room. We head out of the casino and I start to walk toward the elevator.

"Our night is far from over." Mikael says.

"Where to now?" I ask.

"We have a VIP table at Daer. When I brought Hannah here, the bouncer recognized me, and let me know if ever came back to let him know."

We head to the club. Mikael sends a text when we get there, and we're quickly escorted inside by the owner. He takes us to a reserved table down front and brings us a variety of craft beers to try. We've been there for about half an hour when the owner walks onto the stage and grabs a microphone.

"We have a very special treat for everyone tonight. Welcome to the stage Stardust."

Judd and I watch as Dean, Andy, Mikael, and Johnny head to the stage. Dean takes the microphone.

"Thanks for having us tonight. We're here in Atlantic City tonight to celebrate our friend's upcoming wedding. Damien, get your ass up here. You too, Judd!" Dean says.

"Is this cool?" I ask Judd.

"Of course, let's go." he says.

Judd and I walk up on stage and stand off to the side. The guys start playing a cover of the Stones classic Paint it Black. Dean motions me to the mic stand. He and I sing the song as a duet as the crowd goes wild. We do a couple more hard songs then Dean addresses the crowd again. "Time to slow it down for all you lovers out there."

Before they start, Judd motions Dean over and says something.

Dean heads back to the microphone. "We have a very special treat for you now. Making his debut, Judd Walker."

Dean walks over and stands with me side-stage. "I hope this goes okay." I say. Dean nods. The band starts playing Whitesnake's Is This Love.

Judd grabs the microphone and says, "This one's for Mel."

My jaw drops. I look at the rest of the guys and they all have the same look. Judd starts singing and holy shit, he's amazing. I had no idea. And holy shit, that bombshell. He finishes the song and rejoins me. The guys do a few more covers then we all head back to our table. Nobody wants to address the elephant in the room, so we just keep drinking until all the beer is gone.

We decide to head back to the suite, as it's now almost five. We all sleep until Dean's cell rings around 11 to let him know the limo's downstairs. We check out and head down to the limo.

"Um, can I ask a favor, guys?" Judd asks.

We all nod.

"Could nobody mention to any of the girls what I said at the club?"

We all nod again, and I can't shake the bad feeling this is going to blow up in all our faces. I just hope that Lexi agrees I had no choice when she finds out. I start thinking about Lexi, wondering how their night went.

Chapter Fourteen

Lexi

Since our men are all in Atlantic City for the night, the girls are coming over for a sleepover. Everyone's making a dish and we plan on eating way too much food and drinking way too much wine! Mel is coming early to help me get things set up. She arrives around noon with a big glass punch bowl full of my favorite dessert, Death by Chocolate. After we put the bowl in the garage fridge, we head into the kitchen.

"Now you know the real reason you're my best friend." I tease.

"So you've just been using me for my cooking, bitch?"

"Damn right." I say and we both crack up laughing.

"So, what do you think the boys are up to?" Mel asks.

"All the boys, or just the cowboy?"

"Come on, you know how I feel about that topic."

"Fine. I'm not sure what they planned. Truthfully, probably better I don't!"

"I was thinking the same thing."

"Before everyone else gets here, I kinda need to tell you something..." I say.

"What?"

"I may have done something. Well, let Damien do something."

"Well, I'm intrigued."

"I let him take pictures of me."

"And? What's the big deal about, wait, holy shit, do you mean those kinda pictures?"

"Um, yeah."

"Who are you and what did you do with my shy friend?"

"Blame that on a certain sexy rockstar that fucks my brains out."

"I owe him the world for bringing the real you out. I always knew she was in there somewhere!"

"He's incredible, and holy shit, last night. Let's just say my plan worked better than even I thought."

"Deets, please. I live vicariously through you, my dear."

It doesn't have to be that way, I think to myself. I fill her in on Damien's and my antics in the basement and by the end, her tongue's hanging out. Again, I can't help but think that it wouldn't be that way if she'd admit her feelings for a certain cowboy. A little while later the rest of the girls arrive, food in hand, and we take everything down to the basement. Alex takes hers and Hannah's dogs plus Dave and Maggie to her friend Margie's farm so we can just focus on our party. When she returns, I pour everyone a glass of wine.

"Okay, I need to get this out of the way," Hannah says. "I miss Mikael, but I'm actually glad they went. I love night's just hangin' with my badass bitches."

We all clink glasses and chug our wine. We all make up plates of food and sit down together at the table. As we're sitting there eating, Alex says, "I have a game, if everyone's up for it?" We all agree. "Okay," Alex continues, "here's how it works. I'll start by describing my hottest sexual encounter in detail then pick who goes next until we've all shared."

We all agree and Alex tells her story. "For me, it was the night Dean proposed. He took me to Ocean City, Maryland. After his romantic beach proposal, we went back to the house to celebrate. We were both extremely horny that night and we took turns ordering each other around. We fucked for hours, and it was incredible. No man has ever done me quite like him. I'm going to pick the Pet Shop queen, Hannah. I know you have at least one hot one, since I got treated to the audio."

Hannah laughs and elbows Alex. "Mikael is by far the sexiest man I've ever known, so I do have plenty to pick from. Not to sound like a copycat, but there's something about a marriage proposal. When we got home after he proposed, it was hotter than hell. Mmmm, that man. Mel, what about you?"

"Well, I certainly don't have anything that comes close to what I've heard so far, but I definitely hope to someday. I've had decent at best. I think I'll let Lexi tell hers." Mel says. I see a sad look in her eyes and my heart hurts for her.

"Well, for me, it was last night. I gave Damien a night he told me he will never forget. We used handcuffs, oral sex gel, edible massage oil and holy shit, I lost track of how many orgasms I had. Lizzie, what about you?"

"This is an easy one for me! While we were still in LA, Andy took me to a ritzy hotel, well, to have sex! He ordered a make-your own sundae cart and proceeded to eat one off my naked body. That's not all he ate that night! Now, last but far from least, Eden!"

"For me, it was the night that Johnny and I finally admitted our feelings to each other. It took us a while to get there, but when we did, wow! We spent the entire night making love and again the next morning when we woke up together."

After we were done with the game, we grabbed some more bottles of wine. After a few more glasses each, I turn on the stereo and put on a special playlist I made for tonight. I also set up our video camera to record the fun. Cyndi Lauper's 'Girls Just Want to Have Fun' starts playing. We each grab another glass of wine and pretend we're in the video. We're dancing and carrying on when I hear a knock on the garage door.

"I'll get it." Alex says and runs for the door. She returns a few minutes later with a police officer. "Lexi, this cop needs to speak to you."

I walk over and stand in front of him, hands on my hips. "Can I help you officer?" I ask, trying to hide my tipsiness.

"We received a noise complaint. I'll need you to take a seat, please." he says.

Mel brings a chair over and I sit down. The other girls line up their chairs on either side of me and I realize what's going on. Mel turns the stereo off and the "officer" turns his own music on. I hear Poison's "Talk Dirty to Me" start and watch as Officer Sexy shakes his ass in my face. He turns around and unbuttons his shirt. Holy fuck, his chest is broad and muscular. He strips until he's down to a barely-there thong. Damn, looks like he's even bigger than a certain longtime rock drummer who likes to share photos of his cock!

We down a few more glasses of wine each while we watch the show. We're all feeling pretty damn good right now, and our inhibitions have faded a bit - okay, a lot. He pulls me out of chair and stands behind me. I feel his hands on my hips as he grinds behind me. I start shaking my ass as the other girls cheer louder. I hear Lizzie yell conga at the top of her lungs and next thing I know, we're following Officer Big Dick around the basement in a conga line.

When he's done performing, he gets dressed and thanks us for one of the best nights he's had in a while. After he leaves, I lock up the house and go back to the basement. We put the stereo back on and get back to our playlist of fun 80s songs. We all grab a little food and some of Mel's dessert, which includes a good amount of Kahlua. We down a whole lot more wine and we're dancing around the basement, laughing and singing cheesy pop songs at the top of our lungs. It's a good thing our only neighbor is Judd, or we would have actual cops here. We finish all the dessert then we grab a bottle of Fireball whiskey. We do a few shots each. That's the last thing I remember until I hear the loudest noise ever.

Chapter Fifteen

Damien

When we get back, the limo pulls up to my house first. I'm about to get out when I notice everyone's cars are still in the driveway.

"Guys, I think we may want to all get out here. It's well after noon and the women are all still here." I say, raising my eyebrows. Dean pays and thanks the driver and we all get out. I try to open the door but it's still locked. I grab my keys and we all go in. As much as I try to imagine the scene in the basement, I was not at all prepared.

We all quietly walk down the stairs and just stand there staring. There are six beautiful women passed out cold on the basement floor. I see our video camera setup, so I quietly walk over and grab it. I motion for the guys to follow me upstairs. They all take a seat on the couch while I connect the camera to the TV. I press play and the room goes quiet as we sit and stare. We're just about at the end. Mel's the last one to go to sleep. She lays down and we hear her say, "I want you Judd."

After the footage ends, we all sit and look at each other. None of us is sure what to say, especially to Judd, so I finally break the awkwardness. "Well, I don't know about you dudes, but the stripper conga line was the highlight for me!" I laugh. The guys lose it. "I guess we should go wake them up." I say.

"Before we do, I need to say something," Judd says. "You've all been polite enough not to mention last night and what you just heard and I thank you. It's true, I do like Mel, but please know, I'm just not the right man for her, or anyone for that matter."

We all nod, not really sure what to say. Instead, I walk toward the door to the basement. The guys follow me downstairs and watch as I grab the electric guitar I have on a stand in the corner. I turn the amp on and play a couple of chords. They're all standing before me laughing as the six lushes start to stir.

"What the fuck!" Lexi says as she attempts to get up.

"Have fun last night?" I say a bit more loudly than I usually talk.

"Too loud. Too bright. Go away." she says.

I just stand there laughing. The other guys go help their wives up until we get them all sitting in chairs. Judd takes care of Mel, which I'm sure has him conflicted. Despite how hungover they are, how messy their hair and makeup is, and their disheveled clothing, they're still the hottest women ever!

"What time is it?" Alex moans.

"Two." Dean says.

"In the morning?" Hannah asks.

"No, the afternoon." Mikael says.

"You girls need to eat something. We'll be right back with coffee and breakfast." I say.

Other than some moans, the women don't answer. Dean and I go up to the kitchen to get breakfast ready while the other guys clean up the empty wine bottles and the trash that the drunkie-sisters left everywhere. Johnny comes up with a tray of glasses, six wine glasses and six shot glasses.

"No wonder they look like that," Johnny says. "We found six empty wine bottles and an empty Fireball whisky bottle."

Dean and I just shake our heads.

Once the food is ready, we carry everything downstairs. We give each of them a plate of food and a cup of coffee, but none of them are touching the food.

"I know you probably don't want to, but you really need to eat." I say.

They slowly start eating and after about half an hour, finally finish their breakfast. The guys take their wives home, leaving Judd and I to take care of Mel and Lexi. Mel hasn't said a word and she won't look at Judd.

"Judd and I are going to get you home, Mel." I say.

Without warning, she bursts into tears. "I don't want to be alone." she cries.

Lexi moves closer and puts her arm around her friend. Judd and I go stand by the bar. "Talk to me, girl." Lexi says.

I see Mel glance over at Judd then look back at Lexi. "I'm so lonely, and I can't stand it. It sucks when you're damaged goods and no man will have you." Mel says.

I can't help but wonder what she means by that. I look over at Judd and he's looking at Mel with the saddest look in his eyes.

"I've told you before, you're not damaged goods. You have a lot to offer and a woman is more than just that one particular thing. You're smart, funny, beautiful, and the best friend a girl could hope for." Lexi says.

"Thanks, Lex. Can I ask a quick favor?" Mel asks.

"Of course." Lexi says.

"Can I grab a shower before I leave?"

"Of course. Come on, I'll help you get upstairs and get you a towel and washcloth. You're welcome to my shower gel and shampoo."

"Thanks."

Mel grabs her overnight bag and the girls head upstairs. Judd stays and helps me finish cleaning up the basement.

"What do you think Mel meant by damaged goods?" Judd asks.

"I'm not sure, but Lexi seems to know." I say.

"I hate hearing her talk like that," Judd says. "I guess I don't need to tell you I've had some feelings."

"Then why not ask her out?" I blurt out.

"I just can't. She deserves better. And please, don't ask me to explain."

"Got it. Just think about it, though. You heard what she said on the tape."

"I just can't. I'll still take her to the Halloween party, but that has to be it and only as friends."

I nod but don't say anything else. We carry all the dishes upstairs and put them in the sink. Judd heads back to his ranch before Mel comes back down. I hear the shower turn on then a few minutes later, Lexi comes down.

"I'm going to run over and pick up the dogs." I say.

"Okay. I'll just sit here and hope my head stops hurting." she jokes.

When I get back, she's in the kitchen putting the last few dishes away. The dogs come bouncing in and greet her before curling up in their favorite spot on the living room floor.

"Come sit, babe." I say.

We sit together on the couch and wait for Mel.

"Feelin' any better?" I ask.

"A little. Thanks for taking care of me." Lexi says.

"Always, my love."

She lays her head on my shoulder and asks, "So, did you guys have fun last night?"

"We did and I learned something. Judd is one hell of a poker player. We had a private room with a dealer, just playing for fun, and he kicked our asses. We talked about maybe having a game here with all of us. I'd love to see you and him go head to head."

"That sounds fun. Hey, why's the video camera up here? I thought it was in the basement. Oh my god, did you guys watch it?"

"Yep and it was, well, entertaining. There's something I need to show you, but after Mel leaves."

"Okay. I vaguely remember a conga line."

"Oh yeah, the six of you and the stripper. Plus, some interesting singalongs. But, really, it wasn't as bad as you might think." I tease.

Lexi turns bright red. "I'm so sorry we behaved like that."

"You have no reason to apologize. It was just a group of female friends blowing off some steam. It was well-deserved."

"Thanks."

"I do need to show you one thing from your party and one from mine. And you need to promise to keep it to yourself."

I press play on the video and watch Lexi's face as she hears Mel say she wants Judd. Her mouth is hanging open but nothing's coming out. I grab my phone and show her Judd's performance at the club. She looks up at me with tears in her eyes.

"I knew they belonged together. We need to make this happen." Lexi says.

"I know how you feel, but Judd made it perfectly clear that being friends is as far as he'll take it."

"And Mel won't stop believing she's damaged goods."

"Can I ask why she says that?"

"I want to tell you, but I need her permission first. I hope you understand."

"Of course, baby. So, since you're feeling better, do you want some dinner?"

"Yeah, I'm starving."

After we grab plates of leftovers, we spend the rest of the night hanging out in front of the TV then head off to bed. The next couple of weeks, we spend most of our time at the club, getting ready for the Halloween bash. The day of the party finally arrives and I can't wait to see my girl in that sexy costume.

Chapter Sixteen

Lexi

"If you don't get your hot ass outta that bathroom, I'm leaving without you." I hear Damien yell.

"I'm just finishing my hair and makeup." I shout back.

I hear Damien sigh loudly, so I hurry and finish. Before I come out, I yell at him to close his eyes. Once he assures me they're closed, I walk down the hall. When I'm in the bedroom and right in front of him, I tell him to open his eyes.

He lets out a wolf whistle and puts his hand over his heart. "I have a good mind to rip that off you and take you to bed, woman!"

I smile and say, "Just you wait until we get back home. By the way, you look hotter than ever tonight, my sexy T-bird!"

We walk downstairs and give the dogs their dinner before we head out. After they eat, we take them out for a potty break and a quick play session in the backyard. Judd comes over to the fence with a bouquet of yellow roses in his hand.

"I'm off to pick up Mel. See ya both there."

We smile and wave. Once the dogs are done playing, we take them inside. Damien opens the garage door and there's a surprise waiting for me. He bought a '57 Thunderbird convertible in the most beautiful red I've ever seen. I squeal before we get in and head down to the club. There's already a small line waiting to get in and the costumes are awesome. I walk in and smile when I see the staff. Since Damien and I are dressed as Danny and Sandy from Grease, the rest of the staff is dressed either as T-birds or Pink Ladies. I check the VIP table up front, which is reserved for our friends. Everything is all set so we let the first round of guests in.

Figuring that people would want to stay for the entire event, we sold tickets and we completely sold out. The early arrivals head to the bar and start ordering food and drinks. We assigned tables based on the number of tickets sold so everyone has a place to sit and eat. Our DJ, Scott, starts spinning Halloween inspired music. I'm so thankful Cassie recommended him and I'm hoping he'll do our wedding.

Our friends start to arrive and they all look amazing. Andy and Lizzie are dressed as Desi and Lucy from The Lucille Ball Show. Dean and Alex went with Dwight and Angela from The Office. Our superhero nerds, Mikael and Hannah are dressed as Superman and Lois Lane. Rounding out the group are Johnny and Eden who picked Johnny and Baby from Dirty Dancing. A little while later, Judd and Mel arrive as Samantha and Darren Stephens. Mel, however, is more like Samantha After Dark, in a black witch's hat and a black lace dress that leaves little to the imagination. Judd can't take his eyes off of her.

I walk over to the bar and grab pitchers of beer and order some appetizers for our table. Cassie brings the food over herself when it's ready. We all sit down to have a beer and eat some food. The guys don't let us forget our drunken state at my bachelorette party, so we eat more and drink less. After we finish our appetizers, Damien walks up to the stage.

"Thank you all for coming tonight. We're going to have a great time. Before we open up the dance floor, I have a little treat. Lexi, please join me." Damien says.

I walk up to the stage. Damien gives Scott a wave and I hear the Karaoke version of "You're the One that I Want" from Grease start playing. The lyrics come up on the Karaoke machine we have on the stage.

Damien and I belt out the song and we're met with a loud round of applause when we finish.

"Now, let's see all our amazing couples on the dance floor. Scott, let's slow it down."

Bad Company's "Feel Like Makin' Love" starts playing. Damien takes my hand and leads me off the stage to the dance floor. He pulls me in close and I wrap my arms around his broad chest. I inhale deep, loving the smell of his cologne. I feel the heat building between my legs. I lean my head up and whisper in his ear.

"I think I left something in my office." I say with a wink. He practically pulls my arm off. We run upstairs to my office and lock the door behind us. We don't even bother getting completely naked. He sits on the couch and I sit on his lap. We fuck hard and fast, then head back downstairs. The amused looks on our friends' faces lets us know we didn't fool anyone.

I look over and I see Judd dancing with Mel. I can't help but stare. They look like they were made for each other. They both have a dreamy look on my face. I feel myself getting emotional and I try to wipe away my tears without anyone seeing me. But, Damien never takes his eyes off me, so he catches me.

"You okay, sweetie?" he asks.

"I'm happy. Look at them." I say as I nod toward Judd and Mel.

He smiles at me and kisses my forehead. I lay my head on his chest as we dance. Even when the music speeds up, we keep slow-dancing. I love the way it feels when I'm in his strong arms, especially when we're naked. I look up at him. He lowers his head and kisses me with so much passion, I nearly have an orgasm!

We dance for a few more songs then go back to the table. I grab a pitcher of ice water from the bar and pour a couple of glasses. Other than Eden and Johnny, we all make our way back to the table. Those two could dance for hours and they look damn good doing it! After a rest we head back to the dance floor. Scott calls for the crowd to split and one at a time, each couple dances down the line. Of course, the ballroom King and Queen look the best out of everyone.

Once it hits midnight, we stop serving and people start heading out.

Once the last few patrons are gone and our friends have all headed out, I gather up the staff by the bar.

"Thank you all so much for your hard work tonight. The event was amazing and that's a credit to each of you. To say thank you, and because tomorrow is Halloween, I'm closing the bar, and you'll all be paid. And you get a break tonight too! Damien and I will be coming down tomorrow to clean up. Head home, get some sleep, and have a fun day tomorrow."

The staff gathers up their stuff and they all head for the parking lot. Security hangs back until Damien and I finish turning off all the lights. I set the alarm, lock up, and security waits until we're in our car. Damien pulls out of the lot but instead of heading home, he drives us to the park. I hope he's thinking the same thing I am.

"Woman, get that hot ass in this backseat now."

He is and I quickly do as I'm told, eager to have his dick inside me. Damien slides my pants and panties down around my ankles. He unzips his jeans and my favorite plaything pops out. I start laughing and I'm met with an annoyed face.

"I'm not sure I like you looking at my dick and laughing." he scolds.

I snort loud, compose myself, and say, "It reminded me of a jack-in-the box. Except, in this case, it's a cock-in-the-box."

"Oh my god, woman, what am I going to do with you?"

"Fuck me, I hope."

"Climb on, baby. I want you so damn bad."

He grabs my hips and holds me tight as I slide up and down his dick. Fuck, he feels so good. We both quickly explode and I collapse against him, chest heaving. He holds me against him and kisses me hard. I climb off and slide my clothes back up. He fastens his jeans then pulls me back into his lap. We start kissing in the backseat, completely lost in each other until we hear a car pull in next to us.

"Get a room!" Dean teases, earning a playful swat on the arm from Alex.

Damien gives him the finger and we all laugh. "I couldn't wait until I got this hot babe home." Damien says.

"Totally get that, it's why we're here." Dean says.

Alex's face is about as red as mine feels. "The park is all yours!" Damien says.

We get back in the front seat. Damien starts the car and gives the lovebirds an obnoxious honk before we pull out and head home. He blasts the music and we sing at the top of our lungs for the entire read home. We're both exhausted, so we take the dogs out to go potty then we head to bed.

Chapter Seventeen

Damien

A couple of weeks have passed since the Halloween bash, bringing us ever closer to the wedding. But before that, I'm awakened this morning by a sexy woman singing Happy Birthday while two furries are panting in my face. She crawls across the bed to me, giving me a nice look down her shirt. She lowers her head and crushes her lips to mine. Her tongue explores every inch of my mouth and I feel my dick stir.

"After breakfast. I need to run down the club for a little while then grab some stuff for tonight. I shouldn't be too long."

"Okay, baby. What do you want for breakfast?"

"You're the birthday boy, so that's your choice. I'll make you whatever you want."

"Oh, I know exactly what I want, and it's between your sexy thighs."

"You'll have to wait until later, my love." she says with a wink.

I give her a fake pout, but if I know I my naughty woman, she'll more than make up for making me wait. We get dressed and head downstairs.

"I would love an omelet and some rye toast, babe." I tell her.

"Coming right up."

I feed the dogs while she gets the coffee started. I watch her grab what she needs to make me breakfast. When she's done, we sit down to eat. After she cleans up, she heads down to the club and I take the dogs out back. Judd sees me and comes over.

"Happy birthday, man." he says.

"Thanks. Are you still coming tonight?" I ask.

"Looking forward to it. Is Mel still coming?"

"She is." I watch his face as I answer and I swear I see it light up for a second.

"I'm looking forward to going up against Lexi in poker."

"She is too!"

"Is there anything I can bring?"

"Lexi has it covered, but thanks for the offer."

"I gotta get back to work, but I'll see y'all tonight."

"Later, man."

I watch as Judd heads back to his ranch. I get up and grab a couple of tennis balls so the dogs can get some exercise. Lexi gets home a couple of hours later with a couple of grocery bags full of different snacks for tonight.

"Guess what?" she asks.

"What?"

"I got us a dealer for tonight. Cassie heard we were having a poker game tonight and asked if she could deal for us, since it's her night off."

"Awesome. I'm looking forward to the party, but truthfully, I'm even more looking forward to everyone going home."

"Damien, those are our friends. That's not nice!"

"But, baby, all I can think about is what you have in store for me."

"Well, you better behave now or I may not give it to you!"

"I'll be good." I say.

She smiles then bends over the counter and shakes her ass. Fuck, this woman is going to be the death of me. She takes my hand and walks me into the living room. I see a gift sitting on the coffee table.

"Do I get to open this one now?" I ask.

"Yeah. Just look at the tag first." Lexi says.

The tag says "To Damien From The Furries." I tear the paper off and open the box. Inside is a beautiful photo of Dave and Maggie sitting together down by the pond."

"I love this. Thank you so much, baby. When did you take this?"

"After you left for your Atlantic City trip."

"You have a real knack for photography."

"Thank you. I'm glad you like it. Now, I need to get some stuff setup in the basement, then I want to grab a shower."

"Can I help?"

"No way. It's your birthday, so you get to relax."

I watch as she gathers up some bowls and takes them downstairs with the snacks. She comes up a little while later and shuts the door.

"Hiding something?" I ask.

"Nope, but I don't think we want Dave and Maggie having access to the snacks."

"Good point."

"I'm heading up for my shower now." Lexi says.

I follow her upstairs, hoping she'll let me join her. Of course, she doesn't turn that down .We stand in the hot shower together and I have to fight hard not to get an erection. But, our guests will be here soon, so I need to keep junior resting for now. After we're done and we get dressed, we head back downstairs. Lexi carries more stuff downstairs to get set up. I'm in the living room with the dogs when I hear the doorbell.

"Hey, boss." Cassie says with a bright smile.

"Hey, Cass. Thanks for doing this."

"Looking forward to seeing the legend herself play," she jokes. "Where can I set up?"

"That door leads to the basement," I say, pointing. "I'm not allowed down there until Lexi says so today."

Cassie laughs and heads down to the basement. I can't make out what they're saying but I hear them both crack up laughing. I hear more cars in the driveway and look out. I see everyone arriving and entering the house through the garage. I'm almost afraid to see what that woman's been up to down there. I hear someone coming up the stairs. Lexi pokes her head out and calls for the dogs. They come running and go downstairs with her, leaving me just standing there waiting. Once more, I hear someone coming up. The door opens and Dean walks over to me with a blindfold.

"Come with me to the garage," he says. "That way, it's only a couple of steps down."

He puts the blindfold on me and leads me down to the basement. He walks me to where I assume Lexi told him to. He pulls the blindfold off and I can't believe my eyes. There's a huge banner wishing me a happy birthday, but what really catches my eye are all the pictures hanging on posterboards around the room.

There's pictures of us with the dogs, pictures from different things we've done together. No, not those things, including some awesome shots of all of us from the Halloween party. One picture in particular holds my gaze and I feel tears forming.

"Who took that one?" I ask, pointing.

"Me." Mel says with a big smile on her face.

I can't stop staring at the picture of Lexi and I sitting on a bench at the dog park. We're gazing at each other and the look on both of our faces is pure love. Mel couldn't have captured a more perfect moment. Lexi walks over and gives me a big hug. She follows it with a sexy kiss, not caring that our friends are all watching. I hear wolf whistles from the guys and clapping from the girls. After a round of birthday hugs and handshakes, Lexi stands next to the food tables.

"Thanks for coming to celebrate with us. Before we eat, I wanted to check with everyone and their Thanksgiving plans." Lexi says.

"I've already been uninvited from the family dinner, so I'm free." Mel says. Lexi squeezes her hand. The rest of the group all also let Lexi know they have no plans.

"Well, you all do now. Damien and I would love you all to join us for a day of fun, food, and football. Now, please, help yourselves. Cass, that includes you!"

After we all finish eating, Cassie sets up the poker game. She sets a stack of chips at each of the ten chairs and gets the cards out. We all take our seats and she explains how the tournament will work.

"As each of you runs out of chips, you're eliminated. We'll play until we have just one winner. The game, of course, is Texas Hold 'Em," Cassie explains. "Lexi, you get the honors."

I have no idea what she meant by that but Lexi the poker queen clearly does as she smiles wide then shouts, "Shuffle up and deal."

Everyone's smiling and chatting except for Judd and Lexi. The stone faces on the two of them are almost scary. One by one, the two sharks pick each of us off, until they're the only two left at the table. Their chip counts are almost identical and I can't even begin to guess which one of them is going to win.

The room is silent other than Cassie's instructions as she deals hand after hand. I'm mesmerized by how focused the two of them are and how seriously they're taking a tournament that's just for fun. Cassie deals the flop, turn, and river. The board now shows the ace of spades, the eight of clubs, the queen of diamonds, the queen of spades, and the two of hearts. Judd looks at his hole cards and I see the slightest change in his expression. He pushes all his chips in and declares, "All in."

Without hesitation, Lexi responds with, "Call."

"Players, please wait until I've counted both stacks," Cassie says. She quickly counts then announces, "Lexi has a slight chip lead, so if she wins this hand, she wins the tournament. Judd, please show your cards."

Judd has an ace and an eight, giving him two pairs. Lexi shakes her head, a smug look on her face.

"Seriously, dude," she says to Judd. "You called with the dead man's hand?" She flips her cards over and my jaw drops. I see the queen of hearts and the queen of clubs.

Cassie's grinning from ear to ear as she declares Lexi the winner. She and Judd both stand. He walks over and shakes her hand. "You're one hell of a player." he says.

"You were one tough opponent," Lexi says. "But you should know that hand is cursed."

Lexi explains the legend of Wild Bill Hickok being killed while holding that hand. She references a scene from one of her favorite poker movies, All In, where the main character's father loses with that hand.

"I've heard that," Judd says. "And now, I believe it."

Cassie starts cleaning up the poker chips and cards. "Now that we're done, I'll head out." she says.

"You're welcome to stay if you'd like." Lexi says.

"Thanks, but I'm going to head to the club and hang out with Scott while he DJs, if that's okay."

"Of course." Lexi says. She walks Cassie out and I take a seat on the couch. When she comes back to the basement, Lexi stands behind me and whispers, "I want you."

It takes every ounce of restraint not to throw everyone out. Just thinking about being naked with her makes my breathing shallow and I start panting like Dave. Lexi grabs Mel and they go to the garage. They return a few minutes later. Mel is carrying ice cream, while Lexi has a cake with lit candles. The group sings happy birthday then Lexi and Mel give everyone cake and ice cream.

"Damn, dude, what did she say to you?" Mikael teases.

"Uh, nothing, why?" I answer, trying but failing to sound casual.

"So, nothing has you panting right now? Sure, dude." Mikael says.

Everyone else laughs. I know damn well I'm not fooling anyone. The guys all know how hot that woman gets me, and I would be shocked if the girls hadn't shared stories about us. A little while, everyone starts to head out and the guys don't hold back on the ribbing. I barely notice as my mind is completely occupied by very dirty thoughts. Once the last of our guests are gone, Lexi turns to me, hands on her hips.

"Get your ass into the bedroom. NOW!"

Chapter Eighteen

Lexi

I laugh as Damien races up the steps and into our bedroom. He stands in the room but doesn't move. I give him a wicked smile and a wink, causing his tongue to spill out of his mouth. I love having this effect on my man!

"Okay, birthday boy, you will get to do whatever you want to me tonight, but first, I have a treat for you. First, I want you naked and on the bed."

Damien quickly removes his clothes. I lick my lips as my eyes explore his sexy body. He lies down on the bed.

"Good. Now, my only rule now is that you are not allowed to play with your dick."

He gives me a puzzled look, but soon, he'll understand why I said that. I grab my phone, open my favorite music streaming app, and play Sheena Easton's Sugar Walls. I stand at the foot of the bed and lock eyes with my sexy lover. I swivel my hips as I slowly pull my shirt over my head, revealing a sheer, black bra. His eyes go wide as he watches me dance while I teasingly slide my jeans down.

His eyes go right to my black lace panties and I see a couple drops of drool forming. He moves his hand toward his dick, but I wag my finger.

"If you touch that cock, I get dressed."

His hands grip the bedspread as he watches me. I turn and bend over to remove my socks and sneakers, giving him a view of my ass. I turn around and pull a chair to the spot where I was just standing. I sit down then spread my legs wide.

"Holy shit, woman! Have you been wearing those all day?"

"Yes, babe. I bought them just for tonight." His eyes refuse to leave my panties. Or, in this case, my pussy, since I'm wearing crotchless ones! I watch his face as I unhook my bra and slide it off. I leave the panties on and lie down next to him in bed. "Now, my sexy birthday boy, I'm yours for the rest of night. I'll do anything you want me to. Your wish is my command."

"Oh, Lexi, this is easily the best birthday I've ever had! Now, I want you on all fours with that pretty mouth wrapped around my dick. I want to come in your mouth and watch you swallow me."

"Mmmm, my pleasure, sexy!"

I get on all fours and take every inch of my sexy man down my throat. I hear his groans as I slide my mouth and tongue up and down his erection. I tease his balls with my fingers and feel his hand lightly swat my ass. I feel his balls tighten as he gets close to coming. I feel him fill my mouth and damn is he delicious. I look into his hungry eyes as I swallow him down.

"Fuck that felt so good," he growls. "Now I want to taste you. Get on your back, baby. And leave those hot panties on."

I lie down and open my legs wide.

"That's my good girl. Get ready for a tongue lashing like nothing you've ever felt."

Just hearing those words from his sexy voice nearly make me come undone. He gives me a wicked look before his head disappears between my thighs. I feel his tongue slide the entire length of my pussy and I writhe beneath. He alternates between sucking and licking harder than ever before. My entire body's on fire as the pleasure becomes almost too much to handle. I scream as I explode with one of the strongest orgasms I've ever had. I lose all control of my mouth.

"Holy fucking shit, you sexy fucking stud. That felt so fucking incredible." I cry out.

"Mmmm, you taste so damn good, woman. Now, get that hot, wet pussy around my dick. I want to watch those hot tits bouncing while you ride me. I can't stand another second not being inside you."

Damien lays back down. My legs feel like jelly after that orgasm, but I manage to make them move and I mount my sexy rockstar. I take him all the way inside me and fuck, he feels so good. I sit up straight, giving him the view he loves and start rolling my hips. I feel him twitching inside me, getting me even hotter.

I start fucking him harder, bouncing up and down on his rock-hard dick. His groans get louder and he matches me with strong thrusts that quickly send me into orbit. I come hard, drenching his dick.

"Fuck me hard, baby."

He pulls me down against his chest and holds me tight in his arms while I pound his dick hard.

"Oh god, Lexi, I love you so much." he growls as I feel him empty inside me. He keeps me in his arms, our chests heaving together, his dick still inside me.

"I love you more than I ever knew was possible, Damien." I whisper breathlessly.

"Do I still get more birthday wishes?" he asks.

"I told you anything you want."

"Then what I want more than anything right now is a relaxing soak in the tub with my woman next to me."

"That sounds perfect."

I walk down to the bathroom and turn the water on to start filling the tub. Damien joins me and climbs in. I'm about to do the same when he laughs at me.

"What's so funny?" I ask.

"Uh, you still have your panties on."

"Yeah, you told me I had to leave them on."

"Okay doofus, I meant while we were in bed." he says.

"Oh, well, you didn't say that." I tease. I slide them off and sit down next to my man.

"Now, get that hot, wet body in my lap. But this time, I want you in reverse cowgirl."

I slide over and carefully lower myself down on his cock, which, of course, is hard yet again. He pulls my back against his chest and starting with my boobs, he runs his hands down my body. He teases my clit with his fingers as I grind against his cock.

"Oh, this feels so good." I moan.

"Mmmm, baby." he whispers in my ear, giving me chills from head to toe.

He keeps his arms around me. I put my hands over his as we move together in the water. I've never felt as much love from anyone as I feel from him tonight. Just the thought that I get to spend the rest of my days loving and being loved by this man fills my soul with the peace I've always sought.

"Alexis, please turn around and face me. I need to see your beautiful face when we come together."

He never calls me by my full name, and I love the way it sounds rolling off his tongue. I lift off of him, turn around and reclaim my place in his lap. He wraps me in his arms as we lock eyes. We move together as one until wave after wave of pleasure overcomes our bodies. Completely spent, I collapse against him. His hands cup my face as he kisses me tenderly. We stay like this until we can't stop yawning. We dry off, drain the tub, and after taking the dogs out for their last potty break of the night, head straight to bed.

Damien turns off the light and pulls me close. "I know I said this earlier, but thank you, my love, for the best birthday I've ever had." He kisses the top of my head as I drift off to a blissful night's sleep.

We spend the next couple of weeks getting more work done on the wedding, including sending out invitations. Part of me still can't believe this is my life, but it is and it's fucking amazing! About a week after the invitations went out, I'm in my office at the club when my cell rings. I see Billy's name pop up on my screen.

"Hello," I say.

"Hi Lexi, Billy here. How are things?"

"We're doing well. More importantly, how are you?"

"I'm coping. I miss Jack so much."

"I'm so sorry. I wish there was more I could say or do."

"Just having you and Damien as friends is more than enough. And Damien is exactly who I wanted to talk about."

"What's up?"

"I'm definitely coming to the wedding, but I was thinking I'd like to surprise him."

"That would be great. What'd you have in mind?"

"I'll send back a decline, as if I have to work or something, and then surprise him."

"I love that idea. Just let me know your meal choice and I'll add you to the count."

"That's perfect."

"I have another idea, if you'd be willing?"

"What?"

"I don't have anyone to walk me down the aisle."

"And you want me? I would be honored."

"I think it would be a fitting tribute to Jack and it will help Damien deal with things."

"Thank you, sweetie, for helping with this. Damien's lucky to have you."

"Thank you. I'm lucky too."

"I need to run, it's almost time for me to leave for work. I can't wait until I see you both again."

"I'm looking forward to it. Have a wonderful Thanksgiving."

"You as well."

"Goodbye, Billy."

"Goodbye, Lexi."

I can't help but smile as I disconnect the call. Now I just have to keep Damien from finding out. I have one more thing to take care of before I head home. I walk to the top of the stairs and call for Scott. He comes up and takes the seat across from me.

"Is everything okay, Lexi? I hope I haven't done anything wrong?" Scott asks, a concerned look on his face.

"Not at all. You're very good at what you do, and that's why I've asked you up here. I would love to hire you to DJ for Damien's and my wedding, if you don't already have plans for New Year's Eve."

"I don't and I would love to do that. But, really, it's not necessary to pay me extra."

"Don't be silly. I will absolutely be paying. Please tell me what you would normally charge for a wedding."

"I could never charge you that much."

"If you don't tell me, I'll just check your website." I say with a smile.

"Normally, one thousand."

"Done. You're hired."

"Thank you so much. I promise you won't be disappointed. Do you know what you want in terms of music?"

"Damien is handling that, so he'll be touch base with you."

"Great. Thanks again."

"You're welcome."

Scott heads back downstairs. I pack up my stuff and head home. I need to start getting things ready for Thanksgiving. It's only a week away and I have a lot of work to do. But for tonight, I plan on just relaxing with my man and our dogs.

Chapter Nineteen

Damien

I wake up the morning of Thanksgiving and I'm alone in bed. I hear noise coming from the kitchen, so I head downstairs. I walk into the kitchen and stop dead in my tracks. Lexi's standing there in pajamas, her hair up in a messy bun, getting the turkey prepped. Watching her clean out the bird activates my primal instincts and I've never wanted her more. I just stand there grinning at her when she looks over.

"What the hell, dude? I'm up to my arms in turkey yuck and you look like you want to fuck." she says.

"I've never seen you look hotter, woman."

She rolls her eyes and says, "Oh my god, Damien."

"Seriously, though, what can I do to help?"

"I'm almost done with this part. Once I get cleaned up, you can help me get the stuffing ready."

"Then do I get to stuff you?"

"Honestly, Damien! You're insatiable."

"That's all your fault for being so fucking sexy."

That earns me another eye roll but this time it comes with her bright smile. Damn, I love this woman. She finishes up and puts everything she's getting rid of into a bag. She walks over to the sink and cleans up her hands and arms then grabs what we need to make the stuffing. We sit down at the kitchen table and she gives me my instructions.

"After we're done with this part and I get the turkey in the oven, I'll make us breakfast." she says.

"Wrong answer, woman. I'll be cooking breakfast."

"I don't mind cooking."

"I know, sweetie, but you're making this amazing meal for all of our friends, so the least I can do is cook breakfast."

"Well, then I won't argue. Thank you."

As we work on breaking up the bread, I see a somewhat sad look on Lexi's face. "You okay, baby?"

"Oh yeah. Just thinking."

"Tell me."

"Well, this holiday really means so much to me. That's why I wanted to do this today."

"Can I ask why?"

"Of course, silly. I know you've already seen my parents in action. Well, they always hosted all their ritzy friends for dinner. That meant that their embarrassment of a daughter had to stay hidden. My grandparents hated the way they treated me. My grandfather would pick me up the night before and I would spend the night at their home. The next morning, my grandmother would get me up early and I would help her prepare the family meal."

I see tears start to form in Lexi's eyes as she continues.

"My grandparents would always invite their friends that had no other family. We always got complimented on the food and it was nice to feel like I belonged somewhere. Even when it was only Mel and I, I would still prepare a smaller scale meal for me and her. So, I'm on the emotional side today, really missing my grandparents. They would have loved you."

I lean forward and kiss Lexi on the cheek. I take my thumb and wipe her tears off her pretty face. I'm about to get back to breaking bread when she glares at me.

"What?" I ask.

"Go wash your hands before you touch more food," she commands. "My grandmother would have yelled at you for that!" she smiles.

After I pass inspection, I come back to the table and we finish up. Lexi puts in the rest of the ingredients for the stuffing and now it's time to mix everything.

"What spoon do you want to mix?" I ask.

"Oh no, no. I have so much to teach you," she teases. "Watch and learn."

I watch her put her hands into the bowl and start mixing everything together. She looks at me while she works. She starts moving her hands slower, adding a little hip grinding to it and my dick starts to stir.

"Get your hands in here and help me." she says.

I join her in the bowl, watching her face as she works and damn my pajama bottoms are suddenly a bit tighter. I move my body so she can see me. She looks down and shakes her head. After everything's mixed, I get a lesson on jamming bread up a turkey's ass. I watch as she rubs butter all over the outside of the turkey. I walk over to her, stand behind her and rub her sexy ass.

"Oh yeah, rub that meat for Daddy!" I say in my sexiest voice.

"Damien St. James, honestly!" she laughs. "And by the way, your damn dick is poking me in the ass!"

She finishes the prep on the turkey and gets it in the oven. We stand together at the sink, washing up and all I can think about is her naked ass on the counter.

"Now that you've got the bird in the oven, how 'bout you let me put my bird in your oven. Get your ass on the counter."

"What am I going to do with you today? We have people coming over. I am NOT having sex on the damn counter."

"Fine. Get back to bed then."

She wags her finger in my face. "Do you have any idea how much I have to do to get ready? That will have to wait until after everyone leaves, mister!"

"Well, damn, I've been told," I laugh. "Now what would you like for breakfast?"

"Just some scrambled eggs and toast. I want room for dinner."

"Coming right up."

After we eat and clean up, I get more marching orders and we get the rest of the food prepped. Everything left has to wait until later. Lexi goes upstairs to shower and of course, I'm hot on that sexy little tail.

"Now that we have some time to kill, please baby, I need to be inside you!" I say. Before she can answer, I pull her in close and crush my lips to hers. I feel her melt against me as she moans into my mouth. I feel her hands slide down my pants and stroke my dick. She pulls me over to the bed.

She takes her pajamas off and is about to take out her bun when I stop her. "Please, that looks so sexy, leave it in." She smiles and lays on the bed. She wags her finger, signaling me to come to her.

"I'm already soaking wet for you. Please get that cock inside me and fuck me hard."

I fuck her hard and fast, both of us quickly coming undone. We get in the shower together then get dressed in jeans and Eagles jerseys. She's especially excited today since the Eagles are playing the Cowboys. Or as she calls them, Cowgirls. We head downstairs. Lexi goes back into the kitchen, so I join her to help. Our friends will be here soon for the game then dinner.

Judd's the first one to arrive. He has a bouquet of flowers in his hand. He walks into the kitchen and greets Lexi then hands her the flowers.

"Thank you for inviting me, Lexi. These are for you."

"Wow, that's so sweet. Thank you."

I grab a vase and put the flowers in water so Lexi can keep cooking.

"I'm all set here, so why don't you guys relax before dinner," Lexi says.

"Are you sure?" I ask.

"I got this."

As everyone else arrives, Lexi shoos them all into the living room. I notice that Mel stays with her to help. I take the pies that Eden brought and put them in the garage fridge. I check on Lexi one last time, but

Mel's helping her, so I join the others in the living room. I see Lexi open the oven to take the turkey out, so I go help her. She lets it rest as she gets the rest of the meal into serving bowls, which Mel and I help her carry into the dining room.

Once everything's on the table, she hands Mel a bottle of wine to pour everyone a glass. She gives me the water pitcher and I take care of that. I return to the kitchen to carve the turkey and carry the tray to the dining room. I escort my love to the table then stand at the head.

"I'm so grateful to have this amazing group of friends to enjoy dinner with. I need to give a special thank you to Lexi for this amazing meal." I raise my glass and everyone follows suit. We all toast then start passing the food around. After we've all eaten way too much, Lexi gets up to start clearing the table, but I stop her.

"You worked so hard today that I want you to sit and enjoy the game," I say.

She gives me a tired smile and says, "Thank you."

The guys all help me clean up while the ladies sit in the living room and ogle the players in their tight uniforms. When we're done cleaning up, we join the women for the rest of the game. By the end, Lexi is yawning uncontrollably.

"I'm so sorry for yawning so much. It really isn't any of you," she says.

Everyone tells her they understand and thanks her for the meal. About an hour after the game ends, everyone gets ready to head home. There's so much food leftover that Lexi sends everyone home with another meal. When everyone's gone, she flops down on the couch, her eyes drooping. I take the dogs out for their last bathroom break then we head up to bed.

We're lying together, holding each other. "Thank you so much for today. The food was amazing and I loved spending the day with all our friends," I say.

"Thank you for the help, and the sex," she smiles.

"Hey, do you realize in only a little more than a month, you'll be Mrs. St. James?"

"I can't wait. I love you so much."

"I love you, baby."

I give her a tender kiss and watch as her eyes close and she drifts off to sleep. I settle in next to her, the last thing I remember until morning.

The End...for now.
Stay tuned for the exciting conclusion, Rockin' Winter, coming December 21, 2022.

Acknowledgments

Cover Designed by Carter Cover Designs
Proofread by Zoejayne Knight

About the Author

Samantha Michaels was born in 1973 in the small town of Abington, PA and was raised and still lives in Hatboro, PA (both suburbs of Philadelphia). She is married to her high school sweetheart and they have a rescue dog, a beautiful Black Lab named Holly.

When she's not writing or working at her full-time job, she enjoys watching her Philly sports team (hopefully) win, listening to heavy metal/hard rock music, Texas Hold Em, reading, and spending time with friends and family.

Her love of reading began at a young age, thanks to her mother and Sesame Street. Her mom read to her constantly, and by three years old, she was reading on her own, and hasn't stopped. This eventually turned into a love of writing. She was writing for herself and then for a small group of friends, one of whom told her she should be writing books. She took her friends advice and has since published several romance books with plenty more on the way.

Newsletter: https://forms.gle/zB4pXvdgETJJHm5FA

www.ingramcontent.com/pod-product-compliance
Lightning Source LLC
Chambersburg PA
CBHW020154180626
46810CB00004B/1884